Green Mountain Sapsuckers

and

SapNet

Green Mountain Sapsuckers

and

SapNet

by

Harry Goldhagen

HarryLlama Media
PO Box 61
East Fairfield, VT 05448
www.harryllama.com

Onion River Press
191 Bank Street
Burlington VT 05401
www.phoenixbooks.biz/onionriverpress

Table of Contents

Preface

While driving down the highway to Burlington with my brother one warm spring day in 2013, I began complaining about the sorry state of vampire movies. What had happened to the wonderful gothic horror story Bram Stoker had given the world? The evening before I had watched another variation on the theme, Daybreakers, and I was disgusted. The concept of the movie, corporate vampirism, and the incessant and annoying blue tint of the film (among many other script problems), was just too much for me. As I paused for breath during my tirade, my brother quipped, "If vampires ever came to Vermont, they'd bite maple trees."

The vision of fanged green creatures creeping through our maple woods was too enticing to resist. "That's it!" I shouted.

And so Green Mountain Sapsuckers was born. For some reason his joke sufficiently inspired me to create this romantic, silly story. The plot emerged nearly fully formed during that trip, including two of the main characters, Charlotte St. Johnsbury and Dr. Milton Fairfax.

Sapsuckers was just what I needed to distract me from the weight of the day-to-day struggles we were facing. That was a dark time. The preceding winter, my brother had barely survived a life-threatening illness and the medical mismanagement that made things so much worse, and we were still searching for a way to get him better. Luckily, just a couple of weeks before, we found a specialist who would eventually unlock the answers and put him back on the road to health. That hadn't happened yet, but we were starting to feel hopeful.

Who understands the vagaries of the writing spark? Most of my screenplays took months or years to plan and write, with many breaks and pauses and doubts. Perhaps the hope the specialist gave us freed up my creative voice. Maybe it was the Terry Southern books I was reading at the time. Southern is barely remembered now, but he was a brilliant, hip satirist in the '60s and '70s, best known for his screenwriting with Stanley Kubrick on Dr. Strangelove and with Peter Fonda and Dennis Hopper on Easy Rider. I was astounded by Southern's wild, free-wheeling approach. Nothing was too sacred for his searing wit to skewer. Though our styles differ enormously, his uninhibited voice gave me the encouragement to write how I liked.

Or maybe it was Vermont itself. I moved to the brave little state around seven years before, and it now felt like home. I knew almost all the neighbors who lived on my dirt road, at least to wave to, and I attended most town events, like Jig in the Valley, and Trunk or Treat, and the concerts at the repurposed, rehabilitated old church, The Meeting House on the Green. I had accumulated enough warm clothing to get me through the winter, which really made a difference. Beyond that, I had a network of friends and colleagues, writers and actors, sugarers and sauerkraut makers, vegetable farmers and music teachers. And underlying all of this were the rolling mountains and the thickening forests, fully clothed in summer, bare in winter. These small homey villages and towns and hopeful little cities were filled with people I was glad to know. I had found my home, and it had become a part of my life, an important character in my story.

Whatever the reasons, I was inspired and energized. I worked on the Sapsuckers script daily, whenever I could squeeze in time while waiting for appointments with doctors and technicians and physical therapists, and within two weeks I completed my first draft. Shortly after, I had a better version. I showed it to a few close friends and family, made a few changes, had an enjoyable reading with some local farmer-actors at the Flack Family Farm, made a few more tweaks, and voila! The screenplay was done.

But what next? The scale of the script was beyond the meager resources of my film production company, HarryLlama Video. Local filmmakers liked the script but had no time or money to take it on. Local theater companies were not interested. I even submitted to Amazon Video, but, without a big name attached, it didn't have a chance. So the script sat on the shelf. I dusted it off every so often to reread it, but it was waiting to be brought to life.

About a year ago I read an article in the paper about Phoenix Books and their new self-publishing arm, Onion River Press. Why not publish the Sapsuckers screenplay? I could include a few other funny Vermont scripts I'd written to fill out the book, like Kaleanation and The Veggie Underground. I gave a call to Rachel Fisher at Phoenix, and we got the ball rolling.

But then a friend asked, "Who reads screenplays?" I

couldn't argue with that. I had enough trouble getting people in the film and theater world to read the script. How would regular readers take to it? I did a quick search on Amazon for screenplays, and found that there weren't very many. Most, in fact, were "how-to" books: Write Screenplays That Sell, How Not to Write a Screenplay, How to Write a Screenplay That Doesn't Suck, this person's method, that school's approach, etc., etc. The rest were scripts from well-known films like Chinatown, the Harry Potter series, Taxi Driver, Titanic, and the like. I doubted anyone would take a chance on a script by an unknown writer for a yet-to-be-made film.

"So make a novel out of it," my helpful friend continued. "How hard could that be?"

It seemed very hard, at first. A movie script is like a thumbnail sketch in some ways. All the dialogue is there, of course, but only brief descriptions of the scene, the mood, the lighting and the costumes. None of the blocking, that is, where people stand and how they move and gesture. All that gets worked out during pre-production (and sometimes during the production!)

"But you have the scenes in your head. Just describe them," he finished.

So that's what I've done. I looked through the imaginary camera lens I carry in my head and wrote what I saw. I listened to my characters' internal voices and wrote what I heard. I peered into my characters' hearts and wrote down what they felt. Although it took longer than two weeks, it was still a manageable, creative, and even enjoyable endeavor.

During this process I grew to love even more my brave, daring couple. What could they do next? This prompted me to write a second novella about them, this time without a screenplay as a basis. SapNet began with a kooky idea I had while taking my daily walk. My house is surrounded by maple woods, and pretty much every tree has a tap and a sap line attached to it. "If only these sap lines could hook up to the internet," I thought, "I could stream movies without them continually pausing and stalling." These thoughts led me to the Internet of Things, the ongoing connecting up of every device and appliance, every house and office and car, so that we can monitor everything everywhere from our smart little phones. From there it was only a short step to SkyNet, the malicious, interconnected entity from James Cameron's Terminator movies.

I hope you enjoy these two novellas. (And if any filmmakers or theater producers are interested, I still have the script....)

Harry Goldhagen
East Fairfield, Vermont, 2019

Acknowledgements

It takes many people to make a village, even one as small as Skunk Hollow. I'd like to thank all the people who helped make this book possible. My brother, Michael Goldberg, for starting the whole shebang, and for proofreading the manuscripts and layouts. Thanks are also due to Doug and Barbara Flack for their wonderful enthusiasm and support, and for organizing the first reading by a number of talented actor-farmers around their delicious kitchen table.

Thanks also to Rachel Fisher of Phoenix Books and Onion River Press for guiding me through the process of publishing my first book, and for making sure that everything was correct before going to the printer.

The poem recited in the ritual scene of Green Mountain Sapsuckers was adapted (with apologies) from Song: The golden apple, by Alfred, Lord Tennyson.

The many arboreal poems recited in SapNet by Dr. Woodford include Trees, by Joyce Kilmer, Song of the Trees, by the Christchurch, New Zealand poet Mary Colborne-Veel, and Stopping by Woods on a Snowy Evening, by Robert Frost.

The "sappy" classic tune that Dusty Rhoades sang is based on Summertime, from Porgy and Bess, music by George Gershwin, lyrics by DuBose Heyward and

Ira Gershwin.

I first read the memorable phrase "pullet surprise" as the title of a gruesomely enjoyable "Bug of the Month" column by Larry I. Lutwick, MD, and Edward K. Chapnick, MD, from the January 1997 issue of *Infections in Medicine* (referring to psittacosis, I believe). I have since learned that "Pullet Surprises" was the title of a 1969 book by Amsel Greene about her students' enjoyable malapropisms.

The artwork was created in Photoshop Elements 2019, and I must acknowledge the pithy, spot-on tutorials by David Asch, author of How to Cheat in Photoshop Elements 12 (unfortunately now out of print) and his online videos on the same subject. As a fan of open-source software, I used Open Office for writing and editing the novellas and Scribus for layout and desktop publishing. The text was typeset in Garamond No. 8. I used Irfanview to review illustrations and photos.

Photo credits:

The photomontage illustrations in this book were made from photographs, clip art, and other digital images found here and there. All photographs were taken by the author except where noted. Other digital elements were from stock image sites (Pixabay, my favorite, unless noted otherwise), as listed below.

Cover and page 36: Illustration by **Katie Simpson**. simpsonk06@gmail.com
Page 5 & 63: Photo of Studebaker by WikimediaImages.
Page 6: Photo of sky by Ashish Bogawat.
Page 10: Photo of Modern Diner, Pawtucket, Rhode Island by Improbcat, from Wikipedia.
Page 15: Photo of the interior of Modern Diner by Carol M. Highsmith, Wikipedia.

Page 18: Digital recreation of the interior of Modern Diner by Jerric Cayas. Page 25: Photo of beer bottle by Tabble. Wood back wall by jjamitis. Wood table by Daria Yakovleva. Spray bottle (aerosol can) by OpenClipart-Vectors.

Page 30: Photo of birch bark by ClassicallyPrinted.

Page 31: Photo of salad bowl by Rockledge Farm Woodworks. Wood table by rawpixel. Wood back wall by jjamitis. Garlic by PublicDomainPictures. Page 42: Image of top hat by OpenClipart-Vectors. Maple syrup jug (and syrup!) from my neighbors, the Trudell Family Farm. Page 44: Image of barn by Joe Alfaraby. Chicken coop by fda54. Broken egg, mop and calf by Clker-Free-Vector-Images. Milk can by PublicDomain-Pictures. Milk bottle by OpenClipart-Vectors. Center illustration by Mohamed Hassan. Background quilt pattern by Danielle Papanikolaou. Page 47: Photo of maple jar by Jody Parks. Dresser by OpenClipart-Vectors. Funny cows by Alexas Fotos. Background tapestry pattern by Estelle Heitz.

Page 51 & 104: Snake head (viper) by Clker-Free-Vector-Images.

Page 57: Photo of The New York Times newsroom in the 1940s by Marjory Collins, from Wikimedia. Photo of the New York Herald Tribune from the 1940s from Wikipedia. Photo of antique typewriter by Alexander Lesnitsky. Photo of old desk from Levenger.com.

Page 61: Circuit board (arduino) by Seven_au. Smart phone by coffeebeanworks. Tree by Deedster.

Page 67: Mesh network topology image by FoobazSVG-Hazmat2 from Wikimedia.

Page 76: Photo of the Duke of York pub, Belfast from Wikipedia. Skeleton by Wolfgang Eckert.

Page 81: Well by theosthinktank. Angry eyes by Clker-Free-Vector-Images. Photo of maple tree by Bob Jensen, Trinity University.

Page 86: Plaid pattern by wicopee. Grass (tennis court) by Pexels. Cakes and pies by congerdesign, fruhed, WikimediaImages, pixel1, and Andrea Hamilton. Background hill by Peter Linforth.

Page 94: Smartphone and hands by geralt. Photo of forest by Evgeni Tcherkasski.

Page 96: Forest photo by Thomas Rackow.

Page 104: Forest photo by SylviaP_Design.

Page 115: TV by OpenClipart-Vectors. Tree face by Clker-Free-Vector-Images.

Back cover: Photo of author by Matt Bucy.

Green Mountain Sapsuckers

Chapter 1

It was a crisp, clear, beautiful spring day, a welcome change after months of unbroken greyness and bone-numbing cold. The late afternoon sun was shining, almost bursting from the shockingly blue sky. Although buds had not yet appeared on the trees, a barely detectable reddening on the narrowest branches hinted that life was once again returning to the frozen north.

As he tooled along the dirt road in his rusty, old but dependable pickup truck, Chester Arthur took in the scenery as if he, too, had been in hibernation and was now seeing the world with freshly opened eyes. He looked around happily at the patchwork of woods and pastures, the occasional rambling farmhouse and weathered, gap-sided barn. There was still snow on the ground, but it was thin and patchy and would soon be gone. Threaded throughout the bare woods were the ever-present sap lines, the life blood of the town and perhaps the whole state.

Chester hummed along with the old time music playing on the local radio station, the kind of country songs that his father and probably even his grandfather had listened to. He was heading home after a long day of physical labor, but he wasn't in a hurry. He was enjoying the spring weather and the scenery. He'd been driving these roads for as long as he could remember, but each spring was like the first time. Now in his 30s, he looked every bit the country boy with his plaid shirt, khaki pants, and camo baseball cap. He was in good shape from all his outdoor work and hadn't yet developed the midline paunch so many of his friends in town sported.

Passing yet another sap-lined sugarbush, Chester thought back to his childhood days, when he would help his family make syrup once the daytime temperatures broke above freezing. He'd drag a sled from tree to tree, pouring the mildly sweet, watery sap from the galvanized pails hanging from maple taps into the big bucket on the sled. He'd drag his sled to the trail, adding his bucketful to the enormous gathering tank on the horse-drawn sled, his father leading the team.

Of course, sugaring wasn't like that anymore. Now it was stainless steel collecting vats, reverse osmosis extraction systems, computer-controlled boilers, and sap lines running to every maple tree. Even though he still liked the old ways of doing things, he could understand using the new technology to save time and make more money. At least that was the idea, although there never did seem to be enough of either.

The music on the radio ended and the news began. Chester usually didn't pay much attention to news reports. If there was anything important to know, someone at the gas station, the local gathering spot for all the country boys in town, would be certain to tell him.

He reached over to turn off the radio when something caught his attention. He turned up the sound.

"And to repeat, some disturbing local news," the announcer intoned. "There has been a series of break-ins at some of the sugarhouses in Merrifield, including the largest, Branagan's."

"Holy smokes," Chester exclaimed, "that's right down the road!"

The announcer continued. "Torn sap lines, broken buckets, and hundreds of gallons of syrup stolen. This is the largest theft in Merrifield history. We hope there's a speedy solution to this outrage. Anyone with information should call the town constable. Now for the WSAP weather report...."

Chester turned off the radio and continued driving along the narrow dirt road, looking for the sugarhouse. Maple syrup theft! Unheard of in this small town. Maybe he could pitch in and help them repair things.

Out of nowhere, a woman's scream rang out.

"Help! HELP!!!"

A woman burst from the woods, running at full tilt. Chester could hardly believe his eyes. She was young, probably in her 20s, and her blond hair, worn in a loose pony tail, streamed out behind her. She wore stylish jeans and a button-down, long-sleeve shirt, with the sleeves rolled up neatly. Chester thought she looked too well dressed to be running for her life across a hayfield.

A pack of some dog-like creatures -- too large for coyotes -- ran out of the woods behind her and began giving chase. They were barking and growling, though they didn't sound like any dogs Chester had heard before. Probably some new cross-breed mutt of some kind, he thought. They were closing rapidly on the woman.

Chester jammed on the brakes, sending gravel and dirt flying. The young woman heard the noise and made a beeline for the truck. Not bothering to wait for an invitation, she pulled open the squeaky door, hopped in, and slammed it shut.

"Quick! Get us out of here!" she shouted.

That was all Chester needed to hear. Without hesitation he revved the engine, but before he could get the truck in gear, the dog-like creatures caught up and surrounded the car. They banged on the doors, growling and vocalizing. Chester thought it sounded almost like speech, as if they were saying "My Queen! Come back, my Queen!"

Looking in the side view mirror, Chester saw that they weren't dogs at all. They were human! People, running on all fours, dressed in woodsy green clothing, with leaf litter in their hair, patches and smears of green on their faces, and especially large, green, rather scary canine teeth.

"What... what's...?" Chester stuttered.

"Go! Just go!" the young woman urged.

Chester rammed it into gear and gunned the engine. More gravel flew. The creatures gave chase, continuing to growl and make frightful faces as they ran alongside the car. They tried to keep up, but Chester, accelerating quickly, left the creatures in the dust.

They sped down the narrow dirt road, sliding around turns, flooring it in the straightaways, leaving a plume of dust in their wake. They passed a dairy farm, where a herd of Holsteins watched them drive by, chewing their cud, unfazed.

Chester was driving fast, concentrating on the road, too busy to talk. The young woman was breathing heavily, looking back over her shoulder, worried.

Chapter 2

They finally reached a paved road. Speeding past a sign that read, "Welcome to Merrifield, Home of the Maple Festival," the young woman said, "I know where we are. Quick, make a left here."

"Here?" Chester asked, seeing nothing but trees.

"Yes, here!"

He made a hard left onto what looked like a cow trail, but luckily there was a road, narrow and rutted, with an old, rickety covered bridge directly in front of them. He accelerated, but he wasn't sure the old bridge could take the weight of his truck.

"Through there!" she insisted.

He down-shifted and drove into the bridge, faster than he liked. The side mirrors barely cleared the opening. The timbers of the bridge floor creaked and groaned but held firm. The engine made a dull, reverberant sound in the dark, enclosed space. A few shafts of light seeped through the spaces in the siding, illuminating the plentiful dust raised by the truck. Chester glanced around in wonder at the massive truss work supporting the bridge, held together with only large wooden pegs.

And then they were through, back into daylight, bouncing over the bump where the bridge met the road. He began to accelerate again, when the woman noticed a pull-off, a smooth dirt patch just off the road, and cried, "Here! Stop here!"

Chester jerked the wheel to the right, hit the brakes hard, and skidded into the dirt patch, stalling the engine. A cloud of dust enveloped the car.

They were both breathing hard in the sudden silence. The dust slowly cleared, revealing a perfectly normal scene: a narrow street in a small town, with neat little houses, well trimmed hedges, swing sets, snow throwers. Chester thought he must have imagined things. Dogs that weren't dogs? Large green teeth? But then he looked over at the attractive young woman, who was trying very hard to calm herself, and realized it must have been real. Whatever 'it' was. He was the first to speak. "What... what... ?"

"You won't believe it," she said.

"But what...?"

"Vampires."

Chester was stunned. "Vampires? In Vermont?"

The young woman explained patiently. "Vampires.

Green Mountain Sapsuckers. You know, tree-huggers, only more so. But this is an especially virulent breed. I've never seen them active before sunset. They've been transmogrified by something."

"Something?"

The young woman was thoughtful. "Something... or someone."

"Who...? Who would...?"

"I have no idea," she replied. "Hmmm... it could be..." She trailed off, lost in thought. Then she shook herself and said, "But how rude of me, I haven't thanked you for saving my life."

Chester was embarrassed. "Well, a beautiful girl like you... A damsel in distress... Anyone would have..."

Now that they were out of imminent danger, Charlotte took a good look at Chester. She saw a handsome young man, broad in the shoulders, narrow at the waist, a country boy who was probably comfortable with farm work and machinery. She stuck out her hand and said, "I'm Charlotte St. Johnsbury."

Chester shyly shook her hand and said, "Chester. Chester Arthur."

"Really?" Charlotte asked. "Are you related to the 21st President, the one who was born in Vermont? Not Calvin Coolidge, the other one. You know, the one no one knows anything about?"

"Yes... I mean no. No relation." Chester paused, somewhat ill at ease. He wasn't used to making small talk with women, especially one so beautiful.

Charlotte said, "Well..."

They sat in silence for a few moments, until curiosity overcame Chester's shyness. "So, what were you doing there with those... those... creatures."

"Sapsuckers," she said. "I was doing research on the sugarhouse vandalism. It just didn't seem like the usual teenage prank. And maple thieves typically don't waste time damaging things, they just grab the syrup and run."

Surprised, he asked, "Research?"

Charlotte sat up proudly and announced, "I'm the lead investigative reporter for the Skunk Hollow Echo."

"Wow!"

She looked down sadly and said, "Oh, it's not that impressive, actually. I'm the only reporter for the paper. And it's like eight pages a week. I graduated journalism school only last year." She paused, then her face lit up. "But this story could be a career-maker!"

Charlotte looked over at Chester and said, "I don't know about you, but I'm starving. There's something about facing danger that makes me hungry."

"You've done this before?"

"Well...." She glanced around the road. "Hey, there's a nice little diner in this town. Let a girl buy her knight in shining armor a cup of coffee and a slice of pie?"

Chester hesitated. "Ummm, well, I don't know, I should probably get home..."

"Is there a Mrs. Arthur there?" she asked.

"Yes..."

"Ohh..."

"She's my mother."

Suddenly cheerful, Charlotte declared, "Well, then. Let's have some pie!"

Chapter 3

Main Street, Merrifield was quiet. Too quiet. Chester was used to sleepy rural villages; in fact, he still lived in one. But Merrifield was like a ghost town. There wasn't a soul to be seen, even at the gas station, the usual hub of activity. And the town was dark. Even the smallest villages have a couple of street lights, but Merrifield was nearly pitch black. Weak light came from the windows of the diner, apparently the only open business.

He pulled up in front of the diner, and Charlotte hopped out before he even turned off the engine. She was talking a mile a minute, fired up by her close escape. As Chester held the door for her, she said, "I'm probably best known for breaking the school board scandal, if you remember?"

Chester nodded, though he knew nothing about it. Charlotte didn't notice. "You know, where the secretary was diverting pencils and paper clips and even the children's milk money to her personal account? It was really awful. Children couldn't even attach two sheets of paper together. I got an award from the Governor's office for breaking the story!"

"Uh, wow!"

"Well, actually, it wasn't the Governor, it was the second assistant for media relations, but still..."

Chester nodded again, but he was distracted. Things didn't seem quite right. It was still a few minutes before full sunset, but the diner was surprisingly dark and foreboding, with an odd, greenish light emanating from who knew where.

A waitress stood behind the counter, wearing the typical striped diner dress and apron. She was slowly pouring a cup of coffee for a policeman sitting on one of the stools. She glanced up at Chester and Charlotte and gave them a subtle, knowing, Mona Lisa smile. The heavy-set, middle-aged policeman looked over his shoulder with a bored look and nodded at them.

The cook had his back to the counter, grilling something smoky. Whatever it was, there was loud sizzling, and flames occasionally rose above his head. He glanced over his shoulder and grimaced at them, then quickly turned back to the grill.

Two old farmers, grizzled and weather-beaten, sat quietly in a booth at the rear of the diner, sipping coffee and eating pie.

Charlotte hadn't noticed any of this. She continued to chatter away. "There's nothing like rural life, is there? I always hoped I could earn a living and raise a family in the country, surrounded by woods and pastures, once I've found the right country boy to share it with..."

They were standing at the front of the diner. The waitress said to Chester, "Be right with you, sugar. Take any seat in the house."

They sat down in the first booth, and Chester took a better look around. He was fascinated by the signs on the walls listing the house specials. Maple-glazed burgers. Maple-battered fries. Maple-flavored apple pie. Charlotte picked up the very small menu and said, "Look at all the maple specials!"

She showed him the menu. It only had five items:

MERRIFIELD DINER

MENU

MAPLE BREAKFAST	$2.99
MAPLE LUNCH	$3.99
MAPLE DINNER	$4.99
MAPLE DESSERT	$1.99
MAPLE SNACK	$1.49

*Genuine Merrifield
Maple Syrup
available
upon request!*

Chester said, "It's a bit, um, unusual."

"I probably shouldn't tell you this," Charlotte said, conspiratorially, "but maple syrup is my weakness, my secret vice. It's the fastest way to this girl's heart."

"Um...well..."

Charlotte stretched back in the padded bench seat, relaxing. "Isn't this diner comfortable? They don't make them like this anymore."

"I'm sure that's true!" Chester said with feeling. He looked around again at the strange, otherworldly surroundings.

"So, what were you doing on that road?" Charlotte asked. "Besides rescuing me?" Her eyes twinkled at him.

"I was heading home by the back route. I just finished splitting a half cord of wood, and I helped a friend repair his tractor."

"So you're good with your hands?" She realized what she'd said and blushed deeply. "I didn't mean that the way it sounded!" she said through her hands, covering her face.

Chester seemed to miss the deeper meaning. "Well, yes, I guess I am. I can fix almost anything. I guess you'd call me a handyman of all trades." He sat up a little taller in his seat. "I can run a rototiller, I harrow and plow. I cut down trees, chop and split them and sell them by the cord. In the winter I put on the snowplow and clear driveways and roads, and pull cars from ditches."

Charlotte had dropped her hands from her face as she followed this list with great interest. "Why, that's wonderful!"

"I suppose." He slumped back down. "There aren't many regular jobs here, so I do whatever I can get."

She saw nothing wrong with that. "It must be very satisfying to be so skilled at so many things. Just like my dad." She looked wistful. "Sometimes it seems the hardest work I do is sit and type."

Chester smiled gratefully at Charlotte. "Thank you," he said, and he meant it. It wasn't every day that someone appreciated his work. She smiled back.

"And what about you?" he asked. "Do you live around here?"

"I grew up just outside of town," she said. "My mother was a Branagan, like the sugarhouse." Charlotte grew thoughtful as she reminisced. "I used to love visiting my grandparents during sugaring. The crackling of the wood, the bubbling of the sap." She paused, as if she could still hear the sounds. "I remember the delicious aroma and the utter sweetness of freshly boiled syrup. We used to pour it on snow and eat it by the bucket!"

"Doesn't get better than that."

"In my senior year, I was voted Queen of the Maple Festival. My mother sewed a beautiful white gown, and the photographer from the local paper took lots of pictures of me. My mom still has the clippings somewhere, but that was a long time ago..."

The waitress walked over with an order pad and said, "Can I get you folks some coffee?"

Chester hesitated. "Um, sure."

"Is it maple flavored?" Charlotte asked.

"Why, that's right, honey," the waitress said. "Will that be with maple crème?"

Chester looked over at Charlotte, who nodded. "With, I guess."

Charlotte added enthusiastically, looking at Chester, "And two pieces of maple pie?" Chester nodded, a bit reluctantly. All this maple was a bit much for him.

The waitress said, "That's my favorite. À la mode?"

Charlotte asked breathlessly, "With..."

"That's right," the waitress answered gleefully, "maple ice cream!"

Chester shook his head and said, "Don't your customers get tired of maple syrup on everything?"

The waitress sighed as she finished writing the order on her pad. "Tired? Honey, we just give folks what they want. And this town just loves its maple syrup. Why, we're even thinking of changing the name of the town to Mapleville!" She turned toward the grill and yelled, "Cookie, that's two icy slices, two white cuppa, pronto!"

The cook turned to face them, grimaced, grunted agreement, then turned back as the waitress strolled back to the counter.

Chester leaned over the table and whispered to Charlotte, "There is something really odd about this place."

"I agree," Charlotte whispered back. "It must be all the flatlanders who've moved to town. They so love anything that says 'Vermont,' no matter how kitschy.

Why, have you seen those silly glass maple leaves filled with about a thimbleful of syrup for $15? I mean, unbelievable, right?"

Chester looked over at the policeman, who picked up his sugar-dusted, maple-glazed donut and took a big bite. Maple syrup gushed out, flowing onto his hand and sleeve. He turned to look at Chester, syrup dripping down his chin and onto his jacket. It looked like blood.

The policeman smiled evilly at Chester, revealing elongated canines. Chester was terrified. He looked in turn at the waitress, the cook, and the old farmers, all of whom stared at him intently with similarly evil grins and long teeth.

Charlotte hadn't noticed the change. "It's like that restaurant in California, you know, the one that serves everything with garlic, even the ice cream, and let me tell you..."

Chester grabbed Charlotte's hand mid-sentence and hollered, "They're here!"

Charlotte, surprised, asked, "Who?" She looked around but saw nothing odd. Everyone looked like they did when they walked in.

Chester shook his head, trying to clear it. "The whachamacallum's, the slapsackers!"

"Snapsuckers... I mean, Sapsuckers," Charlotte said. "Where?"

Chester looked wildly around at the now relatively normal scene, feeling bewildered. "Uh, I don't know, I thought I saw something." Maybe it was his imagination. After seeing those dog creatures race from the woods, who could blame him?

The waitress banged down the coffee mugs and pie, startling them both. She said brightly, "Here ya go!

Enjoy!"

Chester couldn't believe his eyes. The servings were enormous, nearly a third of a pie each, with at least a pint of ice cream dripping over each slice. Charlotte said, "Wow! That's a lot of food." She grabbed her fork, looked over at Chester and said, "Dig in!"

She clearly took her own advice, eating bite after bite and washing it down with coffee. Chester looked worried. He poked the pie with his fork, as if expecting something to jump out.

"This is really good pie," Charlotte said brightly, diving in deeper. "You should try some."

Chester looked up, only to see everyone in the place grinning evilly again. They were creeping closer, as if preparing to pounce. Chester grabbed Charlotte's arm hard, with a look of fear.

"Charlotte!" he cried.

She looked at him in surprise. "My, aren't we forward." She patted his hand. "But that's what I'd expect from a country boy. When he knows what he wants, he just grabs it. But just like we train a bull in..."

Chester gasped, "It's..."

The diner denizens now stood closely around the hapless couple, breathing heavily, smiling evilly. Charlotte was still focused on her pie. She took another bite and said, "You look so funny. What is it?"

"It's... it's..."

Charlotte looked up and finally noticed the evil crowd surrounding the table. "Oh my God, it's the Sapsuckers!" she cried. "Help!!"

Chapter 4

Just as the Sapsuckers closed in on the pair, the door burst open in a flash of light. Glinting silver flew through the air. Chester thought the flying objects looked like throwing stars, something a Japanese ninja might use, only these were in the shape of maple leaves. He watched one fly past and land smack in the center of the cook's forehead. The cook groaned and collapsed onto the floor, where he began to steam and melt. He quickly disappeared, leaving a large puddle of maple syrup where he had stood.

A lumberjack strode through the door of the diner. Chester and Charlotte gazed at him in amazement. He was tall and broad, with wild reddish-blond hair. He was dressed in worn overalls, a red flannel shirt, and duct-taped hiking boots. A red bandana held his hair off his face. He wore holsters on his hips, but instead of guns he carried a spray bottle in one and a metal something in the other. More silver maple leaves shone from two bandoleers crossing his chest. He looked serious.

The policeman reached for his gun, but the lumberjack quickly pulled out the metal something or other. Chester couldn't believe it, the guy was holding up half of a waffle griddle! He held the griddle in front of him like a crucifix and thrust it towards the policeman's face. The policeman recoiled as if he were hit and covered his face with his hands, smoke seeping through his fingers. When he removed his hands from his face, the griddle pattern was burned into his skin.

The energetic lumberjack jumped forward, holding a wooden mallet and something that looked like a stake. Surprisingly, he hammered the wooden object into the policeman's chest. Chester was astonished to realize that the stake was in fact a wooden spile, the kind of spout he used to tap into maple trees to collect sap.

The policeman looked down in surprise. Once the spile was firmly placed, the lumberjack hung a galvanized bucket on it and opened the stopcock. Steaming maple syrup poured out of the policeman. He began to deflate, like a balloon slowly leaking air, until he disappeared behind the bucket. It clanked loudly as it hit the floor. Chester leaned over and peered into the steaming bucket. He thought he could just make out a hint of the policeman's face in the foam.

The waitress was quietly sneaking up on the lumberjack, preparing to conk him on the head with the stainless steel coffee pot. "Watch out behind you!" Charlotte shouted.

The lumberjack spun around while reaching for

the bottle on his hip, which he extracted in one smooth movement. He aimed carefully and sprayed. Charlotte could see the mist as if in slow motion, approaching the waitress' face. The droplets made contact, and the waitress screamed in pain. She covered her face with her hands and screamed, and then ran out the door, steam streaming from her. Charlotte thought she heard a splash, similar to the sound the cook made when he dissolved.

The lumberjack swiveled toward the old farmers, who were standing by their table, frozen. They took one look at him and ran out the back door. He glanced around for more Sapsuckers, but seeing none, he reholstered his spray bottle and waffle iron. He had the self-satisfied look of someone who's pleased with his work. "That should hold 'em for a while," he said.

Charlotte, in awe, asked, "Who are you?"

The rangy lumberjack walked over to their table and held out his hand to shake, first with Chester, then Charlotte.

"Tim's my name, Tim Burr. Kind of the local peacekeeper in these parts."

Chester said, "I'll say!"

Tim looked down at the table and noticed that some of the food had been eaten. "Uh oh, who ate this?" he asked.

"I did," Charlotte answered cheerfully. "It was really quite tasty, although a bit too much maple, even for me."

"Why, what's wrong?" Chester asked worriedly.

"No time to explain," Tim said. "We've got to get this little lady back to my cabin, pronto." He asked Charlotte, "Can you walk?"

"Why, of course I can walk!" Charlotte stood but almost immediately collapsed. Tim reached over and picked her up, throwing her over his shoulder like a sack of potatoes. She seemed ready to complain but then passed out. Tim pivoted and moved rapidly towards the door. "Better hurry, we don't have much time," he called over his shoulder to Chester. He ran through the door with the unconscious Charlotte, pony tail bouncing.

Chester, still dazed by the fight and all that had happened earlier, slowly stood up. He reached for his wallet to pay the bill. Then he shook himself, as if waking from a bad dream. "What am I doing?" He hurried out the door after them.

Chapter 5

Chester ran into the road and stopped short. There was no sign of Tim or Charlotte. He felt the chill of the evening now that the sun had set, and deserted Main Street was even darker and more threatening. The few storefronts were blacker than night, and even the gas station was closed, with only a few glowing lights from the pumps. Chester shivered, but whether from the cool evening or from facing the Sapsuckers he couldn't tell.

Then he heard running steps. He caught a glimpse

of Tim way down the street, turning onto a side road. Charlotte hung limply over Tim's shoulder. Chester started running to catch up, but he was very far behind.

Just as he reached the side road he saw Tim carry Charlotte into a small cabin about a quarter mile ahead. Chester jogged to catch up. All the houses were dark, without even the glow of TV sets or wood fires. He thought he saw eyes, green-glowing, peek out between drawn curtains, but he wasn't sure, and he didn't stop to look. He kept jogging until he reached the house, where he stopped to catch his breath. It was an old style log cabin, with a wide covered porch, dull tin roof and tall, somewhat tilted chimney. Warm yellow light glowed brightly through the curtained windows and lit the front porch through the open door.

Still breathing hard, Chester stepped inside and halted. He was trying to make sense of the calm scene in front of him. The cabin was surprisingly neat and clean. There was plentiful handmade wood furniture and small colorful rope rugs scattered about. A large black woodstove dominated the center of the one-room house, with a semicircle of comfortable chairs around it. To the left was a well-stocked pantry and a small desk, and a combination kitchen and dining area was off to the right.

Tim was fiddling with some sort of workshop clamp light in the kitchen, attempting to aim it at the dining room table, where Charlotte was lying on a blanket. Her face, even in unconscious repose, was beautiful, although there was an odd, disturbing green tint shading her closed eyelids and shadowing her cheeks and lips. She was wearing surprisingly little, not much more than her rather frilly underwear. Chester began to object.

"Wait a minute, what's going on here?" he exclaimed. "That's no way to treat a... a reporter!"

"Not to worry," Tim said without looking up. He snapped on the fixture and adjusted its direction, illuminating Charlotte in bright red light. "No evil intentions here. It's part of the treatment."

Chester was puzzled. "Treatment? She only ate some pie." He walked towards the table as if in a trance. Mist began rising from her skin where the red light shone.

"Now for the messy part," Tim said. Using what looked like a turkey baster, he dripped some liquid onto Charlotte's face, focusing on the green patches. More steam rose up, and Chester could swear he heard hissing, like boiling maple sap. Tim dribbled a few drops of the liquid onto Charlotte's lips, and she unconsciously licked them and swallowed. He applied the liquid to her lips a few more times, until a massive wave of steam emerged from her skin. Then all became quiet.

Tim clicked off the red light. He bent over Charlotte, examining her face carefully. "I think we might just have caught it in time," he said. "The next few minutes will tell." He turned to Chester, who looked worried, and said, "Get you a brew?"

"Uh, sure."

Tim reached into an old icebox-style refrigerator and pulled out two beer bottles. They had hand-made labels that read "Tim-Foolery Burr Beer," with a cartoon lumberjack in the center. Tim popped off the caps and handed one to Chester, who looked at the unfamiliar label questioningly.

"No worries," Tim said, "I've got my own microbrewery in the barn out back."

Tim took a large swig, then wiped his mouth with the back of his hand. Chester looked suspiciously at the bottle, then shrugged. "Why not," he thought, "it's been a rough day." He looked at the bottle again, smiled at the label, then took a large gulp. He gasped and coughed and spit some out.

"What the hell is this?" Chester sputtered.

"Fermented maple sap, mostly. A few other special ingredients. It's got some anti-sapsucker potency. Like it?"

Chester took another sip, and coughed less this time. Gasping, he said, "Uh, yeah."

Tim took another look at Charlotte. She was sleeping soundly, and her face had returned to its previous rosy glow, with no trace of green.

"I think we saved her," Tim announced.

Chester, not comprehending, said, "Saved her? Saved her from what?" He started shouting. "What is all this? What's going on? I mean, this is crazy!"

Tim took another sip and said, "I 'spect so, to an outsider. But when you've been fighting them as long as I have, nothing seems strange anymore. For instance, your girlfriend here..."

Chester had been taking another sip of the microbrew, but he began coughing and sputtering. "Girlfriend?" he exclaimed. "We met just a little while ago. I barely know her."

Tim looked knowingly at Chester and said, "We're usually the last to know. Anyway, your lady 'acquaintance' here was infected with a very bad bug."

"Infected?"

"Oh, yes," Tim explained, "it's in the maple syrup they use in that diner. Some crazy scientist up on the hill created it."

Charlotte's eyes snapped open. "I shaid sho!" She sounded intoxicated. "It's thoshe rotten schnapshippers... schlapshooters... oh, you know who."

She sat up suddenly and saw that most of her clothes were missing. She was puzzled. "My, my," she said, "what's going on?" She noticed Tim and said, "Hello there, big fella!" She turned to Chester and said, "Well, hello, my rustic Romeo!" She seemed somewhat uninhibited.

Tim said, "You're a very lucky lady."

She was still looking at Chester, and said, "I'll say! Why not offer a girl a drink?"

Chester felt embarrassed. He grabbed a flannel bathrobe from the back of one of the chairs and draped it over Charlotte's shoulders. He looked at Tim questioningly.

"The antidote has a few side effects," Tim said. "It'll wear off soon."

Charlotte stood up, and the bathrobe slid off her shoulders. "Oooops," she said. Chester, turning a painful shade of red, retrieved the robe and put it back on her shoulders. He helped her put it on. "Here, let me... this arm goes here... that's it."

Charlotte said, "What a country gentleman! Let's play bull calf and heifer. It's our first..."

"Umm, maybe later," Chester mumbled. He turned to Tim and said rather desperately, "Tim's explaining what's going on, aren't you?"

"Oh, goody!" she said.

Tim gazed at Charlotte's face and said, "Looks like the antidote worked. Let's see, where was I?"

"A crazy scientist," Chester said.

"That's right, Dr. Milton Fairfax. Two years ago, he started 'helping' the local sugarers by injecting something into the trees to increase their yields."

Charlotte turned to Chester and said, "Wanna check my sap? I think it's rising."

Chester, surprised, said, "What? Um, later, I think." He said to Tim, "And they let him?"

"Let him? They'd do anything to increase their yields. And it worked."

Tim paused to take another swig of beer, then continued explaining.

"But then people started changing, looking a little greenish, a little long in the tooth. They couldn't stop drinking their own syrup. The teenagers were hit the hardest. I found a few sucking on the sap lines, lapping from the buckets, not even waiting for it to be boiled."

Charlotte nudged Chester and said, "Let's play hen and rooster. Wanna see my pullet surprise?" She stopped, wondering. "Oh, my! A journalist with a pullet surprise!" She suddenly started to sag. "I feel sleepy..."

Chester caught her as she fell. He looked around, then carried her to one of the chairs near the woodstove. He gently settled her into one and covered her with a red-checked blanket lying nearby. He looked over at Tim questioningly, who answered, "Everything's fine, she'll be alright. Now where was I?"

Tim gestured towards the chairs, and he and Chester sat down next to the sleeping Charlotte. Tim continued, "Oh, yeah. Luckily, by the end of sugaring the frenzy passed. No one talked about it. Not sure they even remembered. But Doc Fairfax looked very pleased by it all. Each year it's been worse."

Tim stopped to take another drink. Chester asked, "And now? The creatures in the woods? The people at the diner?" He gestured towards Charlotte. "And this?"

Charlotte woke up, confused. She looked around, not recognizing anything. She pulled the bathrobe tighter. "Where am I?" she asked in a tremulous voice. She noticed Chester and awareness began to return. "You saved me... we had pie... and then..." She looked at Tim and said, "and then you brought me here?"

Tim nodded and said, "You're lucky to remember. A few minutes more and you might have been one of them."

Charlotte looked puzzled. "But how...?"

"As I was telling steadfast Chester here, Doc Fairfax genetically altered the maple trees. Anyone who eats the maple syrup becomes a genetically modified Sapsucker."

"A GMS?" Charlotte fumed. "Why, that's illegal in

Vermont!"

"It's worse than that," Tim said in a low voice.

Charlotte exclaimed to Chester, "I knew it was more than a robbery!"

"It's not just here. There have been outbreaks in Maine, Massachusetts, all over New England. Even

Quebec. Our Doc has been a regular Milton Maplesap."

Chester, overwhelmed by the fantastical events of the day and evening, stood up tall. He had had enough. "We've got to stop him!"

Charlotte looked up at him adoringly.

"Glad to hear it," Tim pronounced. "But first we have to get ready."

Tim reached into his shirt pocket and pulled out what looked like a piece of birch bark. He handed it solemnly to Chester. It was a list, written in red crayon — at least Chester hoped it was crayon, and not some other red substance. Charlotte looked over Chester's shoulder.

Attempting to decipher Tim's handwriting, he read, "Apple cider vinegar."

"Sapsuckers can only tolerate sweet things," Tim

said. "That's for sour."

Charlotte attempted the next line. "Cranberry juice."

"Bitter," Tim said.

Chester furrowed his brow. "This looks like garlic."

"For its pungent qualities."

"Kosher salt?" Charlotte wondered out loud.

Tim said, "Hey, you never know."

"Limburger cheese?" Chester asked.

"Yup, it just smells awful," Tim said. "That's good for most anything." Tim finished his beer and wiped his mouth with the back of his hand. "Now you and your little pullet here mix this up while I check the perimeter."

Tim stood up, strapped on some weapons, and headed out the door.

Charlotte turned to Chester. "This sounds awful."

"Well, we saw this stuff in action," Chester replied. "Let's make some Sapsucker repellent!"

As they headed for the kitchen area, Charlotte asked, "Pullet?"

"I'll explain later."

Chapter 6

Chester and Charlotte stood at the kitchen counter, surrounded by bowls, measuring cups, wooden spoons, and piles of ingredients from Tim's list. They both focused intently on the task. Here they were, almost strangers, and yet fate had drawn them together in a way they could never imagine. Chester was glad they had something to keep them busy.

"How much salt?" Charlotte asked. Chester consulted the scrawled list. "Looks like two cups." Charlotte carefully measured the salt and dumped it in the mixing bowl. She glanced at Chester, then quickly looked away.

"I still haven't thanked you enough for saving my life. Twice."

Chester, not used to praise, said, "Oh, anyone would have done the same. Do you have the cranberry juice?"

"Here," Charlotte said. "That's not true, it takes a special kind of person to get involved. Garlic?"

"Just finished chopping it. Here you go." Chester pushed the garlic towards Charlotte, who scooped it up and put it in the bowl. He stopped for a moment to find the right words. Then he began speaking, not taking his eyes off of the bowl.

"Everyone pitches in when the going gets tough. Pulling cars out of snow banks, fixing a broken furnace at 3 AM in the middle of winter. It's just what you do here. They'd do it for you, same as you would for them. Limburger?"

Charlotte picked up the cheese and smelled it, then quickly held it at arm's length. "Ugh," she said. "Let's add this at the end." She became thoughtful. "Anyway, that's what I mean, that rural New England spirit. That's the way you are, and... and that's..." Charlotte turned to Chester, facing him fully. "That's why I love you," she admitted.

Chester, surprised, turned to face Charlotte. He said haltingly, "Me? But... someone as beautiful as you... and we just... and you..."

Charlotte threw her arms around Chester and kissed him passionately. Chester was shocked. Nothing like this had ever happened to him before. What was he to do? She must be mistaken. And then he knew. Sometimes it happens like that, love at first sight. And he knew it was true. He kissed her just as passionately.

Unfortunately, Charlotte forgot that she was still holding the cheese when she grabbed him. Without being aware of it, she pressed the awful mass of dairy into his back, smearing it all over his shirt. They continued kissing, but each sensed that something wasn't quite right.

Charlotte was first to break the spell. "What's that smell? Ugh!"

Chester sniffed the air and said, "It's close by." He turned around to look, and Charlotte saw what she had done. "Oh, no, it's the Limburger."

"What? Where?" Chester asked. Charlotte laughed. "Here, take off your shirt." Chester removed the offending garment, revealing a Chew Lotsa Chard tee-shirt underneath. He held it at arms length. "Yuck," he said. He handed the shirt to her.

Charlotte began rinsing the shirt in the sink. "I'm so sorry, I don't know how that happened."

Chester gazed at her and said, "Don't worry about it... dear."

"Dear?" Charlotte said, choking up. "Oh..." She leaned over to kiss Chester, but she forgot she was still holding the hose. She sprayed him with water before she could reach him.

He was shocked by the cold blast, but then he got a cunning look in his eye. "So that's the way you want it?" he threatened. He picked up a measuring cup full of water and gestured as if he was going to throw it at her.

"No!" cried Charlotte. She reached for his arm to stop him, and they began gently wrestling. The arm hold somehow turned into a hug, and then into another kiss.

Just then a door slammed somewhere. "What was that?" the startled Charlotte asked as Chester held her. He said, "Oh, it's probably just Tim coming back for another beer."

The room suddenly filled with Sapsuckers. Two of them grabbed Charlotte, while a third one conked Chester on the back of the head. He dropped to the floor, helpless but still conscious. In a blur he saw the Sapsuckers pull Charlotte this way and that as she tried to fight them off. She kicked one of them, landing a nice blow. "Good girl," he mumbled. Then Chester's world started spinning until it turned black.

Chapter 7

Chester saw strange blurry shapes, very far away. Clouds, he thought, though they looked too brown. Birds, maybe, brown blackbirds. The shapes approached and receded in a random pattern. Or was it random? He didn't know, and for that matter he didn't care. Let the birds take care of themselves. As long as he was comfortable. But was he? The bed felt hard, harder than he remembered. And his head ached. He should just go back to sleep, it will all be better in the morning.

A blurry white thing passed over his face. Too big for a bird. A hand? Was there an arm, too? The white thing passed back, and then back again. It was a hand! But whose hand? He sensed his own hands. One was touching the hard bed. So it must be his other hand. That's using the old noodle!

Chester's head began to clear. He closed his eyes tightly and then snapped them open. He must be lying on the floor, he realized. "Time to get up," he heard. Did he say that? Didn't really matter, it was good advice. He sat up and felt awful. He rubbed his face and looked around. And then he remembered what had happened.

He stood up quickly, too quickly, staggering, nearly falling over. He grabbed the back of a chair and steadied himself. He looked around and saw chairs and tables knocked over, plates and cups scattered across the kitchen floor. "Charlotte," he croaked. He tried again. "Charlotte!" No answer.

He walked to the door and opened it, looking out into the almost complete darkness of rural Vermont. "Charlotte!" he called again. "CHARLOTTE!" he shouted as loudly as possible. He heard her name echo in the darkness. Where was she?

"Tim!" he called. "TIM BURR!"

"Here I am," Tim said from the back of the house. He walked in and surveyed the wreckage. "She's gone," he said. "They took her."

"We've got to find her!" Chester said.

Tim said, "I think I know where to look. But first..." Tim reached into a cabinet, grabbed a holster belt and bandoleers, and handed them to Chester, who strapped them on. Chester picked up his baseball cap and put it on backwards. He looked menacing. "Let's kick some sap," he said.

Chapter 8

Chester generally enjoyed the forest, day or night. Whether cutting down trees with his trusty chainsaw, racing ATVs and snowmobiles on well-worn dirt trails through the woods, or tapping maples, he spent a good part of his life in the forest. Maybe he couldn't give their latin names, but he could tell you which ones were good for building, burning, or sugaring. The woods were a second home for him.

And yet tonight, as he followed Tim on an unfamiliar, unmarked forest trail, it seemed like a strange, twisted jungle. The woods were dense and threatening. Trees that usually grew straight and tall looked bent and crooked in the light of his headlamp. Long-fingered branches reached out for him, with evil intentions.

He didn't know where he was, or where Tim was leading him. All he knew was that they had to rescue Charlotte, no matter what the danger.

Tim turned to Chester with his finger to his lips. "I see light up ahead," he whispered. "We'll need to turn off our lamps. Just keep close."

They clicked off their headlamps, plunging them into nearly complete darkness. This was the country, with almost no ambient light. They stood, breathing quietly as their eyes adjusted. Tim touched Chester's arm and pointed ahead and to the right, where Chester could just make out a slight orange glow through the tangled trees. "Bonfire," Tim murmured.

They walked towards the glow. Tim was surprisingly light-footed, even in his duct-taped boots. Chester did his share of stumbling, cracking twigs and snapping branches, but managed to keep up. The fear was gone. With the destination in sight, he felt ready.

As the intrepid pair got closer, they could see the bonfire more clearly. It was big. Silhouetted shapes moved in front of the fire, but Chester could not tell whether the shapes were of man or beast, or some dreadful mix of the two. A low whine or a drone of some sort made Chester's skin crawl.

They reached the edge of the clearing and hid behind a pile of split wood. What Chester saw shook him to the core. The blazing fire lit the grotesque scene. In the center stood one of the largest maples Chester had ever seen. Nearly a dozen Sapsuckers danced around it, chanting unintelligible words.

Chester looked more carefully through the heat-distorted air and the shifting shapes of the dancing Sapsuckers. Something wasn't quite right about the tree. Thick ropes were tied around the enormous trunk, holding up a white bundle of some sort.

One of the Sapsuckers danced close to the tree and the bundle jerked away. That wasn't a bundle, that was Charlotte! She was dressed in a white gown, probably the one she wore when she was queen of the maple festival. She was awake, and terrified.

Standing on a stump off to the right was a short, middle-aged man, well groomed and oddly dressed in a tuxedo and top hat. Tim nudged Chester and whispered, "Dr. Fairfax." The doctor looked cheerful, waving his arms as if he were conducting an orchestra.

The Sapsuckers now stepped and danced in a more formal way around the tree, as if performing a ritual. They began to chant:

> The golden maple, the golden maple, the
>   hallowed trunk,
> Guard it well, guard it warily, guard it airily,
> Until the sap is drunk.

They lifted their cups and drank. Dr. Fairfax called, "Sing my children, sing!" They continued:

> The maple sap, the maple sap, forever
>   floweth,
> From the root, drawn in the dark,
> Flowing 'neath the fragrant bark.
> Guard the maple night and day,
> Lest someone come take it away.

Chester whispered, "What's going on?"

"Beats me," Tim said. "I've never seen them like this."

One of the Sapsuckers, who seemed to be more important than the others, danced over to Charlotte. He was wearing a garland of maple leaves, with a matching wreath on his head. He lifted the wreath dramatically and placed it like a crown on Charlotte's fair hair. The Sapsuckers cheered, then chanted again:

> Maple Queen, our Maple Queen, the ruler of
>   our tap,
> Protect the bark, protect the flow, make it
>   grow,
> Guard us from the unforeseen.

The Sapsuckers became quiet and stood still, waiting. Dr. Fairfax intoned, "Now my friends, it is time to anoint this child. Bring the blessed syrup."

The garlanded Sapsucker carried a familiar looking brown jug into the firelight. He held it high above his head, and rotated to show it to all. The Sapsuckers howled and cheered. To Chester it looked like a traditional maple syrup jug. The Sapsucker stepped closer to the hiding pair, and now he could read the label: "Pure Vermont Maple Syrup," it said, with a note in smaller type underneath, "Improved by Dr. Milton Fairfax, patent pending."

"This is horrible," Chester whispered to Tim.

"I suppose," Tim replied, somwhat abstractedly. He seemed to be in a trance. Chester wanted to shake him, but he returned his attention to the ritual.

The garlanded Sapsucker approached Charlotte and showed her the jug, presenting it from different angles, as if expecting her to admire it. She strained at the ropes to get away. The rest of the Sapsuckers gathered at her feet, almost like tame dogs. They looked up at her and smiled, showing their green fangs, but somehow in a less threatening way. He began pouring the syrup, covering her head with the golden liquid. It dripped onto her gown and then to the ground, where the Sapsuckers slobbered and lapped it up. Charlotte cried, "No, not maple syrup. Please!" Charlotte fainted as the lead Sapsucker poured more syrup on her.

Chester said to Tim, "We've got to stop them!"

Tim, still in a trance, said, "Uh huh." Then he began crawling away.

Chester frowned. "Where are you going?"

"Just remembered somethin'," Tim mumbled. He crawled and left. Chester shook his head. It was now all up to him. Charlotte's life was in the balance, and he was the only one there to help. Charlotte had fainted from the ordeal. She hung limply in her bonds against the tree. He had to do something.

Chester jumped out from his hiding place and began yelling, making a frightful noise, waving his arms and kicking his legs for good measure. Anything to stop the ritual. The Sapsuckers jumped, then scattered.

"This can't go on!" Chester shouted. "Flee, you wretched creatures. Go back to whatever tree you climbed out of. Go, or meet your doom!"

He held the waffle iron high over his head. The firelight reflected brightly off the oiled metal, making it glint and glow. It looked like a formidable weapon. The Sapsuckers huddled at the edge of the clearing, howling and whimpering.

Dr. Fairfax stepped down from his stump and cleared his throat. He faced Chester and said in a quite reasonable voice, "What's all the fuss about? A little singing and dancing in the woods? A bit of hocus pocus to keep my followers happy? They want a queen, who am I to disappoint them."

Chester lowered the griddle and pointed it at the doctor. "I know what you've done, Dr. Fairfax. You've taken the solid citizens of Merrifield and made them vampires. Sapsuckers!" The creatures were now huddling around Dr. Fairfax's legs. They moaned at the accusation.

"You don't understand anything, young man," Dr. Fairfax calmly replied. "What did these law-abiding, tax-paying citizens have to look forward to? A life of untreated chronic diseases as the government takes away their health benefits? Poverty in their waning years as they lose their pensions and pay their taxes? I'm saving them!"

"Saving them?" Chester spat out. "By changing them into monsters?"

Dr. Fairfax rested his hand on one of the Sapsuckers, calming him. The others swayed and crooned and held his legs. "Monsters, you say?"

He looked down at his faithful minions and smiled at them. They made cooing sounds. "Look how happy they are. Their lives are filled with nothing but sweetness. They have no more worries about health insurance they can't afford. They don't get sick! They have nice shiny teeth and healthy bodies. They won't get old, so they don't have to worry about losing Social Security benefits. They're happy."

Chester was losing steam. He didn't know what more he could say to convince this man that what he was doing was wrong. He said, "But... but they're..."

"Monsters, you say? I'm afraid you're looking in the wrong direction, young man. The monsters are in Washington, DC. They're in the boardrooms and the penthouses, the state capitals and the fine mansions. They're the ones destroying society. I'm saving it!"

Charlotte had woken up and heard some of Dr. Fairfax's ravings. She said, "You're wrong, Dr. Fairfax, very wrong. You can't save society by destroying it. You can't save people by genetically altering them to suit your purposes."

Tim suddenly stepped into the clearing, dragging a fire hose. "We've had enough of these kinds of solutions. Here in Vermont we look out for each other. And we're not going to stop now!"

Chester shouted, "That's right!"

Tim aimed the hose at the Sapsuckers and opened the valve. A strong stream of beer hit them hard. Steam began to fill the air. The Sapsuckers began to scream, rolling around and sputtering. But to Chester and Charlotte's surprise, they didn't dissolve into puddles of syrup. Instead, something magical happened. They slowly changed back into the rather soggy citizens of Merrifield.

Tim shut off the hose. He folded his arms across his chest and rested one foot on a log. He looked proud of his work.

The former Sapsuckers stood up, looking at themselves and each other in wonder. They didn't know what had happened to them, or why they were standing in the woods soaking wet. Tim said, "You can go home now." Some started leaving the clearing in ones and twos, staggering their way back to town, while others stood or sat around, trying to get their bearings.

Chester untied Charlotte. She threw her arms around him. "My hero, again!" she cheered.

Chester said, "Aw, shucks." She kissed him like she would never come up for air. But eventually she had to catch her breath. She asked Tim, "But what happened? Why didn't they melt?"

"I just finished my latest microbrew," he answered. "Tried a few new ingredients, like citrus and sassafras. Thought it might do the trick." He held out a bottle. "Want a nip?"

Chester and Charlotte, still holding each other, looked deeply into each other's eyes and began to laugh. Chester said, "We're good, man."

"But where's Dr. Fairfax," Charlotte wondered.

They looked around, but he was nowhere to be found. Only his top hat remained, sitting on the stump.

"Looks like he got away," Tim said. He took a deep swig of the beer, then turned to the remaining, puzzled Merrifielders. "Anyone want a brew?"

Chester and Charlotte laughed again.

Chapter 9

Chester gently tossed his head and mooed as he made horns with his hands, index fingers pointing straight out. Charlotte giggled as she moved his piece around the board. "Five, six, seven, eight. You get to visit the heifer barn!"

"Mooooo," Chester bellowed happily, tossing his head again. They were lying on Charlotte's quilt-covered bed in her cozy, rustic bedroom, playing a board game. It was only a few hours since they left the clearing, but they were still energized from the experience. They were dressed as before, with Chester in his Chew Lotsa Chard tee-shirt and khakis, and Charlotte in the maple-stained but otherwise still lovely gown. "Mooo!" Chester intoned.

"My, what big horns you have," she said admiringly, playfully patting his head. She picked up the dice and rolled. "One, two, three. Two extra buckets!"

"I'm being stampeded," Chester complained.

Charlotte stood up and stretched. She said, "I haven't had this much fun playing 'Bulls and Heifers' in years." She walked over to the dressing table and looked in the mirror. "My hair is a mess!" She picked up her hairbrush and began brushing it out.

Chester said, "You do like your barnyard games."

Charlotte looked at Chester in the mirror and stuck out her tongue, then threw him a kiss. "Now that I've got the scoop of the century," she said, "I'm sure I'll get my own byline."

"What's that?"

"My own advice column, 'Ask Ms. Maple.' For people to write in with their questions and mysteries. I'll try to solve them." Looking in the mirror, Charlotte noticed the maple stains on her gown. "I've got to get out of this thing before it sticks to me permanently."

As she headed to the bathroom she looked over her shoulder coquettishly and said, "Now don't you go anywhere, Elmer..."

"Moo," Chester said contentedly. He sat up and looked around Charlotte's bedroom. Candles flickered on the antique wooden dresser, warmly illuminating the light walls and dark wooden furniture. Framed quilt squares and funny photographs of cows' faces decorated the walls. "Nice pictures," he called out.

Charlotte answered from the next room, "Thanks, I took them myself. Up close and personal, that's my style."

Chester noticed a worn paper bag on the dresser. He stood and looked inside. There were a few bottles of Tim's new brew, a silver maple leaf throwing star, and a few other mementos from the day's adventure. At the bottom was a glass maple leaf jar filled with maple syrup. The label was ripped, but it looked like a drawing of Dr. Fairfax.

"Hmmm," Chester said.

Charlotte walked back into the room wearing a comfy short terrycloth robe and not much else. Chester caught his breath. She looked even more beautiful, with her face scrubbed clean and her hair combed out. She caught sight of the glass maple leaf and said, "Now where did you get that?"

"Picked it out of your evidence bag."

"That's dangerous stuff," she warned.

Chester grinned and pulled the cork stopper with his teeth. "We've faced worse today." He gestured at the beer bottles. "Anyway, we've got the antidote right here." He dabbed a bit of syrup on his neck, behind his ears, on his wrists. "Didn't you say maple syrup is the fastest way to your... heart?"

Charlotte smiled ruefully. "Well, I suppose I'd better do a little more... research." She climbed into bed under the quilt and removed the robe. She looked at Chester and tapped the bed next to her. Chester didn't hesitate. He slid under the blanket beside her and they snuggled. He dribbled a few drops of the syrup on her shoulder, and sensuously licked it off. Charlotte sighed sweetly.

"Yum," Chester said. "Maybe these Sapsuckers weren't all bad." He pulled the blanket over their heads and said, "Just a little more." Charlotte sighed, and then said, "Chester, I think you missed, that's not my shoulder... oh, my!" After a bit more snuggling, Chester's head peaked out from the side of the quilt. He wore a mischievous grin that slowly became more devilish. His face was a bit green around the edges, and his canines had grown just a bit longer.

"There's a little Sapsucker in all of us," he said. His eyes glinted with green light as he winked and dived back under the blanket.

"Oh, my!" Charlotte sighed.

SapNet

Prologue

Benny Branagan tucked his half-eaten sandwich into his jacket pocket and limped over to the ATV. His knee was bothering him again, which was no surprise, considering how much weight it had to hold up. "Maybe Mabel's right," he thought, "I should probably cut back on the breakfast sausages. Three should be enough...."

He heaved his bulk onto the seat and turned the key, and the vehicle roared into life. Benny quickly headed for the access trail in the family sugarbush to check the sap lines. Recent high winds, strong enough to knock down trees, might have damaged some of them. He had all the tools he needed tied to the back of the ATV: chainsaw, axe, pruning shears, drills and bits, and spare tubing to replace crushed or torn sections. And a cooler with a few homemade sausage sandwiches and some beers, just in case.

It was late fall, what the locals call stick season. The vibrant autumn colors were gone, but it was still too early for snow. The woods were a study in greys and browns, bare trees silhouetted against a slate-grey sky, surrounded by a carpet of dead leaves. It was a season with the fewest attractions for tourists. "And good riddance," he grumbled as he rode along, "they only clutter up the woods." Even though the sap wouldn't be running until early spring, it was a lot easier to check the lines now, before there was snow on the ground.

Benny was in his late 40s, but he looked younger, with a full head of dark brown, wavy hair and a short, messy dark beard and mustache, giving a youthful look to his moon-shaped face. He was dressed in his usual outdoors outfit, with an unbuttoned flannel jacket, insulated overalls, and cap with side flaps, all in various shades of brown and camo, and all in extra large sizes.

He rode along at a decent speed, bouncing over the uneven ground, looking left and right at the sap lines threaded through the maple trees, checking for problems. Without the leaves he could see much further into the woods. All the lines looked intact so far, although there were plenty of downed branches.

Noticing something odd ahead, he slowed and then stopped abruptly. "Who the heck ran a sap line across the trail?" he complained out loud. He laboriously climbed off the ATV and grimaced as he put weight on the bad knee. Grabbing some tools, he limped over to the line, scratching his head in puzzlement. He'd never seen a line like this. For one thing, it didn't look like any of their blue plastic lines. It was brown and had a more organic look, like woven bark. And there was something sparkly embedded in it. Quartz, or mica? It seemed metallic, like thin wire, which made no sense. "Probably some newfangled equipment from a sap poacher," he thought.

There was nothing to do but remove it. "Well, here goes," he announced to the woods, bringing his pruning shears up to the line. Sparks flew as the blade touched the thin metal, driving him back in surprise. But he was not deterred. He marched purposefully back to the line and clamped down harder with the shears, attempting to cut through in one snip. But the line resisted his efforts, almost as if it were fighting back. Current started to flow through the shears and into Benny, making him quiver and reflexively grip harder. He began shaking as the current grew stronger. His body stiffened, his eyes rolled up, and then some unseen force seemed to grab and shake him, flinging him nearly 10 feet through the air, which was quite something, considering his weight.

Benny landed hard against a stump and groaned. He shook his head to clear it, but he was still dazed. "What's going on?" he wondered.

Then he heard something slithering in the leaf litter to his right. "A snake," he thought, "just what I need now." He had a morbid fear of snakes, even though there were no serious poisonous ones in these woods. Something brushed his left hand, and when he looked down he saw a sap line, brown and sparkly like the one across the trail, slowly wrapping itself around his wrist. "What the hell?" he gasped. A second line crawled onto his right wrist.

Something else tickled his neck. He tried to lift his hand to brush it away but it was pinned to the ground. A third brown line slid across his collar bone and wrapped itself around his chest. Helpless, he was beginning to panic when current began to flow again.

"Why?" he whispered, just before he lost control of his voice. He quivered and shook until he lost consciousness. It wasn't long before his spirit left this mortal coil, to join that great sausage maker in the sky.

Chapter 1

Faint tapping filled the tiny newsroom with sound. Charlotte was intent on her story, typing away at a furious rate, not even bothering to consult her notes. She didn't have to. By now she had attended so many school board and zoning commission and sanitation district meetings, she could write these articles without even showing up. She yawned but kept plowing through. She had a deadline to meet, and she was already late.

She stopped suddenly, frowning at the screen. She had just typed, "And then the most exciting thing that's ever happened in the world suddenly happened." She had no idea what she was talking about. The most exciting thing that ever happened at one of these meetings was when they debated switching milk suppliers for school lunch, and someone objected, and someone else objected to the objection. This wasn't what she had dreamt about in journalism school.

She took her hands from the keyboard and looked over her desk, hoping for inspiration. There she was in her college graduation photo, posing with her parents and grandparents, everyone smiling and happy and proud, her exciting future just beyond the frame. She still looked about the same two years later, she thought, with her shoulder-length blonde hair framing her mildly tanned, lightly freckled oval face. Perhaps her nose was a bit larger than she liked, and her lips not quite full enough. And maybe she'd put on a few pounds since college, but not that many. At least she hoped not.

She looked at the other photo on her desk. She was posing in front of an enormous maple tree, holding a jug of genetically altered maple syrup in one hand, an award in the other. It was after she broke the story of the Sapsuckers that the publisher had given her a pen name, Sugar Maple, and her advice column, Ask Ms. Maple. Her real name was Charlotte St. Johnsbury -- Charlie to friends and family -- but as Ms. Maple she could write stories with some anonymity in a town where everyone knew everyone else's business.

If only she could find another exciting story. Then the sky was the limit. What if she came across a real scandal, one that shook the pillars of government? She'd crack it wide open. She pictured herself typing at a tremendous rate at one of those big, black, old-fashioned clackety typewriters in a large, smoky newsroom, wearing a smart, stylish office dress, a fedora tilted rakishly on her head, a press badge tucked in the brim, stopping to consult her extensive notes in a well-worn steno pad, turning back to the typewriter to smack out another winner. She could see the front-page headline, "Scandal Under the Capitol Dome," stretching across the entire page, and her byline, Sugar Maple, Ace Reporter, in large letters underneath. The acclaim, the parade, the key to the city, and then the Pulitzer award ceremony, an auditorium crowded to bursting with the best journalists and editors of the day, the master of ceremonies announcing, "This year's winner for investigative reporting, Miss Sugar..."

"Maple! Where's that school board story? I need it five minutes ago."

"Coming, boss!" she called out. That gruff voice had come through the barely open door at the end of the room, the office of the Publisher, Randolph

Strafford III. She wasn't sure what he actually did. He rarely left his office, and he was on the phone a lot. She occasionally heard the tap of a golf ball. But he sure seemed important in the three-piece suit and tie he habitually wore.

She dashed off two more sentences to finish the story and then sent it off. "It's done, boss!" she called. She heard his grumble through the door.

Charlotte sat back in her chair and sighed. Another job well done, or at least finished. She gazed at her diploma, mounted on the wall in front of her. It wasn't very far away, only about two feet beyond the edge of her desk. Her chair back was touching the near wall. The other two walls weren't too distant, either. The Skunk Hollow Echo, the eight-page weekly for which she wrote, was a very small operation, although the Publisher had dreams of a media empire, Skunk Hollow International Telecommunications, Inc. She was the lead investigative reporter for the paper -- but then again, she was the only reporter, as well as proofreader, researcher, photographer and coffee pot washer. They sent the articles to a graphics company for layout and printing. All the other jobs were done by part-timers who worked somewhere else, like the accountant who stopped in for a few moments each week to pick up the bills and receipts and to give Charlotte her meager paycheck.

She consulted her notes. As she debated with herself which exciting story to work on next, Mrs. Flanagan's blowout 87th birthday bash or the three Jersey cows that made a daring break for freedom onto the East Road, her phone rang. It was Chester.

"Hi, honey," she said. "Are we still going out

tonight?" Chester was her boyfriend, a handsome, handy country boy who saved her skin more than once, but was more than a little hesitant about moving in with her. She was going to have to do something about that.

"I'll need to stop home first to change," she said. "You know, you can leave some of your clothes at my place to save time if you'd like..." She heard static and mumbled voices, but couldn't make out any words. "Chester, are you there?"

"I'm here, Charlie," he said. "Sorry, I'm in the Branagan woods. It's... it's not good."

Charlotte was having a hard time hearing him clearly. "The wood's not good?" she asked, puzzled.

"It's... Benny," he said.

"Benny? How's he doing? I haven't seen him in months. Is he any bigger?" Benny was her second cousin once removed on her mother's side, and her first cousin twice removed on her father's side. It was a very small town.

"Benny's dead, Charlie," Chester said, sadly. "Looks like a heart attack. But they found something odd nearby. A sap line...." Chester's voice faded out into static and clicking.

"What about the sap line?" she asked. She looked at her phone, but they were still connected. Then she heard a noise that raised the hairs on the back of her neck. It was a voice of some kind, but it wasn't human. It was flat and emotionless. Otherworldly seemed the best way to describe it. The voice said in a mechanical monotone, "Leave... us... alone...."

"Chester," she cried, "what are you doing? You're giving me the willies."

The static faded away, and she could hear Chester's

voice again clearly. "... and it's a new type of line, no one's ever seen anything like it before. I took a picture, I'll send it over. I'm late for a job, gotta go."

"Chester! Wait!" But he was gone. "Poor Benny," she thought. She would miss the sausage king's great barbecues.

Chester's picture of the sap line popped up on her phone. It was blurry, and the light wasn't very good, but it certainly looked different from any line she'd ever seen. Maybe there was a story here. She wondered who could tell her something about this. Scrolling through her contacts, she found an arborist -- a tree specialist -- named Dr. Rose Woodford. She once interviewed her about tree hummers, people who sang and hummed to trees to help them produce more fruit. "Just don't call them whisperers, they can't stand that," she had cautioned. Dr. Woodford was known for her research on improved growth and fruit production in trees that were read poetry regularly. "They especially like Tennyson for some reason," she had said. Charlotte called her.

"Yes?" said a woman with a kindly voice.

"Dr. Woodford? It's Charlotte from the Skunk Hollow Echo. We spoke once..."

"Oh, yes, of course, dear. I thought it was someone else. I've been getting some strange calls lately."

Charlotte sensed something. "Strange?"

"Oh, it's probably just a prank caller, never mind. What can I do for you, dear?"

"Well, I came across an odd sap line, and I've never seen anything like it."

Dr. Woodford perked up and said, "Really? Odd in what way?"

Charlotte looked at the photo again and tried to

describe it. "It looks like it's made from something woody, kind of like basket weaving, and there's some shiny metal strands in it."

"That does sound quite odd," Dr. Woodford agreed. "Hmm, I'm not familiar with it, but it might be part of a new smart tap system. Let me look around here a bit, I think I have a brochure about it."

"Smart taps? What's that?" Charlotte asked. She heard papers rustling, books falling, a loud crash. "Hello?" Charlotte called into the phone.

There was another crash, as if a stack of dishes descended rapidly to the floor and shattered. "Hello?" she called again. Finally, Dr. Woodford replied, "I can't seem to find that folder right now. Where did you see it?"

"My boyfriend saw it at the Branagan sugarbush in Skunk Hollow," Charlotte said. "Do you know where it is?"

"I think so..."

"Well, you make a right off Main onto Church Street, which becomes the West Road after a bit, then you make a left onto Poor Farm Road, another left on Hardscrabble Road, a right on Branagan Road where that barn burned down last year..."

"That's OK, dear, I'm sure I can find it, I know the woods rather well. The trees will help me if I get lost. I can meet you there in about an hour. I've got some saplings in the arboretum that are crying out for some Robert Frost. Send me that photo when you can. Goodbye."

Charlotte started to say "There's something else..." when she heard the connection end. "Oh, well, I guess I'll tell her about Benny when I see her."

Smart taps? Charlotte was unfamiliar with them.

She turned to her laptop and did a search, finding a local company that made them. "Keep Your Sap Flowing!" their web page announced.

A SmarTap looked like a regular maple tap, but with some kind of sensor on it. It had a wireless transmitter that detected drops in sap pressure and sent the data to a phone or computer. "Seems like a good idea," she thought. "What could go wrong?"

Chapter 2

Once the ambulance left, Chester picked up his tools and headed back to his truck. He was going to miss Benny. The guy was always good for a laugh, a beer and a home-made sausage sandwich. It didn't surprise anyone to see Benny gone. The way the guy ate, it was only a matter of time. But he would sure be missed.

He jumped into his old pickup truck and headed down the road. He had been on his way to a job when he found Benny, and now he was late. Not that they'd mind, everyone looked out for each other in the woods. Anyway, they were old friends.

As he drove the narrow, winding dirt road through second-growth forest, he couldn't help noticing how tangled the woods had become. Every tree that could possibly be tapped had a line running to it. "A man could get strangled just running through the trees," Chester thought. It was a lot of work stringing all those lines, so most sugarers left them up all year. Maybe it wasn't as picturesque as galvanized buckets hanging from taps in the snow, but it was way more efficient. Still, it looked like a crazed, mutant spider had gotten loose in the woods.

And today he was going to help add to the mess. Not that it mattered, any work he could get was good. It was hard to make a living in the country nowadays. But he had his misgivings about today's job. They were going to install some kind of tap that talked to your smart phone. Soon, he thought, everything was going to be smart, certainly smarter than he was, and they wouldn't need someone like him anymore.

He saw a truck parked ahead, tilted precariously on the edge of the road to allow just enough room for milk trucks and tractors to squeeze by. Two country boys in worn canvas clothing were unpacking equipment from the back. Chester pulled behind them and climbed out.

"Hey, Chester," the taller one said. "Nice of you to show up."

"Hey, Mike," Chester replied. "Hey, Jimmy."

"Don't pay attention to Mike," Jimmy said. "We heard about Benny. Poor guy."

Mike added, "Yeah, just yanking your chain. Sorry to hear about it."

"It was bound to happen. But it's always a shock," Chester said.

Mike handed Chester a beer. "A toast to the master sausage maker."

"Here, here," Jimmy added.

"The best," Chester said. They silently sipped their beers, paying homage.

After a decent interval, Mike said, "OK, we finished the north woods last week, let's get to work on the Skunk Mountain section in the east." Jimmy and Chester nodded. They each grabbed as much equipment as they could carry and trudged off into the woods, Mike taking the lead.

As they walked through the underbrush, crunching leaves and twigs, Chester started whistling, glad to be working with his friends again. They knew each other since childhood, doing everything together, having adventures and making trouble. Jimmy Flanagan was tall and lanky. He had long, dirty-blond hair and an unruly beard. He thought of himself as a musician, even though he didn't have much talent. He was even in a band, Boyz in the Woods, though they didn't get many gigs since none of them were any good. His friends didn't have the heart to tell him how bad he was. Jimmy wasn't much of a student, either, and he left school as soon as he could, barely squeaking through high school. But he was very handy outdoors -- he had a successful firewood business and a thriving vegetable farm. Chester couldn't think of anyone he'd rather work alongside.

Mike O'Toole was Jimmy's opposite, in looks and outlook. He had dark, straight hair, worn a bit long, with a full mustache but no beard. He had been an average student until he discovered computers. Since then, he had enough training and experience to keep him fully employed doing programming and design work. He had even come up with several devices to help farmers and sugarers. Mike had designed the smart taps they were installing today, and hoped to make a successful business of it.

Chester asked Jimmy, "How does this stuff work, anyway?"

"Beats me, Ches. It all seems like voodoo."

"It's easy," Mike asserted. "It's a distributed, multi-node, redundant wireless network for remote monitoring using a mesh configuration and smart, autonomous, self-healing sensors."

"It's... what?" Chester asked.

Mike stopped to explain. "Here, I'll make it simple." He picked up a stick and drew some lines in the dirt. "Imagine you're standing here, watching a line to see if the sap is flowing. If there's a problem, like a loose tap or a hole in the line, you phone home. That's what these sensors do." He drew a big circle on top of the line. "And if there's something in the way, like a downed branch or a moose, they figure out another way to call home, like through a neighboring sensor."

Jimmy added, "They've got some kind of artificial intelligence."

"Yeah," Mike said, "it helps them predict and react to problems before they happen."

"How can they do that?" Chester asked in amazement. "I mean, how would they know?"

Mike got thoughtful. "I'm not sure about this part too much, AI is kind of a black box, but... let's say a porcupine has been wreaking havoc, going from line to line, chewing here and there, putting holes wherever he wants. Well, the sensors can tell what's

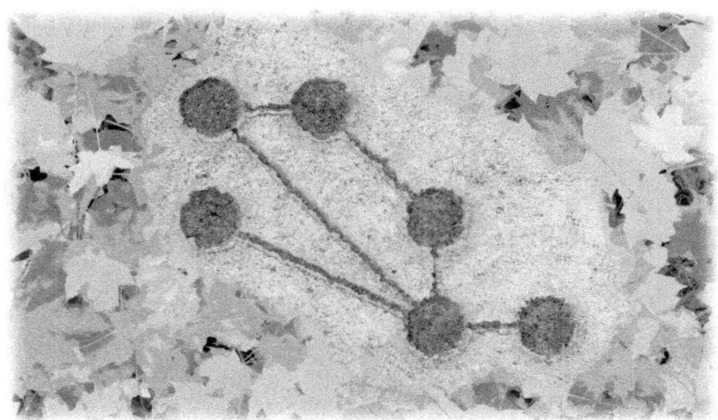

causing the leak by the bite pattern and the height of the leak, and they can track where they're happening. It uses some kind of predictive algorithm..."

Chester's eyes bugged out. "A what?" he asked.

"You know, if you see an ace, deuce, three, four, you might guess the next card will be five."

"If you're lucky," Chester said.

"This is some crazy stuff," Jimmy said.

"As I was saying," Mike continued, "the sensors make a good guess where the next bite might happen -- I mean, how fast does a porcupine move, anyway -- and they run a current through that section of the sap line. Next time that critter tries to take a bite... Zap!"

"Wow!" Chester said.

"I know, crazy, right?" Jimmy said.

As they resumed walking, Chester pondered what he'd heard. It seemed like a good idea, in theory. There were all sorts of animals chomping on the sap lines, like deer, raccoons, porcupines, even the occasional bear. But zapping them? It seemed a little extreme. Maybe it didn't kill them, maybe it gave them just a bit of a shock to teach them not to chew on the lines, like electrified fencing for horses and cows. Yeah, that's probably what Mike meant.

Chester called ahead to Mike, "Where did you get these things? I never heard of them."

"Some guy I went to school with has a side business. He makes the basic units at home. Then I program them to my specs and attach them to the spouts," Mike said. "It's still a work in progress, but once I've got all the bugs worked out, this is gonna be the big one for me. I'm already getting orders online."

Mike stopped at a spot where the ground began to rise. "Here we are, boys. Let's get drilling."

Chapter 3

Charlotte parked her old green Subaru at the site of Benny's last stand, behind an even older, rustier model. It had a bumper sticker that read "Respect Your Elders... and Oaks and Maples." She looked across the field towards the trees and saw a short, roly-poly woman crawling around on the ground near the sap lines, apparently looking for something.

"Dr. Woodford!" Charlotte called. The doctor raised a hand in greeting but kept searching the ground. Charlotte ran up to her and leaned over to look more closely. "Have you found a clue?"

"Ummm, not exactly." Dr. Woodford sat back on her heels and sighed. "I think I dropped my phone somewhere around here." There was a smear of dirt on her round face, across her cheek. She stood up and made a feeble attempt to brush dirt and leaves from the knees of her brown polyester pants.

Charlotte thought that round was the best way to describe her. She was only a couple of inches over five feet. Her dark hair was cut in a short bob that circled her face, emphasizing its roundness. She had a roundish body, too, and with her rather short arms and legs she looked like she might easily roll down the hill with just the slightest push. Even her thick glasses had round lenses.

"Why don't I call your phone?" Charlotte suggested. She dialed, and the missing phone began to ring. Dr. Woodford turned her head left and right, searching. "I think it must be behind me," she said. She turned around, trying to locate the sound. On her second rotation Charlotte noticed the phone in her back pocket. She reached forward and grabbed it. "Here you go," Charlotte said.

"Thank you so much, dear, I'm always misplacing it." She turned the phone off and returned it to her back pocket. "Now let me show you something I've found over there." They walked a dozen feet or so, to a cleared area between two trees.

"There are suggestive traces in the soft soil here," Dr. Woodford explained. "It looks somewhat like mouse trails underneath the snow." Charlotte leaned forward and squinted, but all she saw was a faint trace of something like a fallen branch.

"It looks like there were sap lines or hoses on the ground," Dr. Woodford continued. "I can even see a suggestion of that woven texture you mentioned. But they're gone now."

"Gone?" Charlotte exclaimed.

"As if they were dragged or pulled," Dr. Woodford said. "See this smearing of the pattern?"

Charlotte was puzzled. Who could have taken the sap lines? And why? Was there a sap line thief in the woods? She uncapped her camera and took some photos of the traces, but there wasn't much to see. She looked around and said, sadly, "I think this is close to where my cousin Benny died today. They said it was a heart attack, which was no surprise, but still..."

"Ah, interesting," Dr. Woodford said. "Let's explore further." They walked between the trees, dodging around and ducking under the ever-present sap lines.

"With all the research you've done, you must know a lot about trees," Charlotte said.

"I've only just scratched the surface, Charlotte, I've barely penetrated the bark, so to speak." She stopped in front of a large oak and gestured towards it. "Just think what this magnificent creature has seen in his long life. The poems he could recite, the songs he could sing... if only we could understand him."

"And you've heard the trees talk?" Charlotte asked in disbelief.

"Oh, no, dear, whatever voice -- if one could be so bold as to use the term 'voice' for such a being -- they use to communicate, it's far below our limited senses. The deepest infrasonic growls an elephant transmits through its feet must be like the high-pitched buzz of a mosquito compared to the depth of tree speech. But they can understand us, I'm sure of it." She patted the trunk, and Charlotte could swear she saw a couple of the lowest branch reach towards the doctor.

Without warning, Dr. Woodford stepped back

from the tree, spread her arms, and began to recite:

> I think that I shall never see
> A poem lovely as a tree.

Charlotte watched in surprise. She'd attended poetry recitals at school, but this was deep-felt oration, like a religious experience, inducing an almost trance-like state. Dr. Woodford's eyes seemed to glow with intensity, and the ends of her lank hair began to lift, as if charged with static electricity.

> A tree whose hungry mouth is prest
> Against the earth's sweet flowing breast;

Was it her imagination, or was the tree swaying? Dancing, even? Maybe it's the wind, Charlotte thought, although she felt no breeze. She looked around and saw a group of maples leaning towards Dr. Woodford.

> A tree that looks at God all day,
> And lifts her leafy arms to pray...

And to Charlotte's great surprise, the trees did indeed seem to be raising their branches to the sky. Remembering that she was here to get a story, she grabbed her camera, aimed and snapped a photo, the flash going off automatically under the shady tree. Everything -- the oak, the maples, and Dr. Woodford -- appeared to jump in the sudden light. She stopped reciting as suddenly as she began, dropping her arms. Even the trees appeared to sag. Charlotte thought she heard a sigh echo through the woods.

"I'm sorry," Charlotte said, "I'm still getting the hang of this camera."

"That's OK, dear," Dr. Woodford said. "I don't want to over-excite them. Wild trees need careful handling. They require graded exposure to stimulation like that."

Charlotte was still trying to make sense of it all. "The trees seemed so... so animated, so alive. It was magical!"

"There's nothing magical about it. Trees have very artistic sensibilities, if only one takes the time to listen." Dr. Woodford resumed walking, looking for more sap line traces. Charlotte quickly stepped alongside her.

"What do you think is going on?" Charlotte asked.

Dr. Woodford looked thoughtful. "I've never seen anything like that photo you sent me, so I can't really say without more research. But if I were to speculate..."

"Yes?"

"I'd say there's some malevolent force at work."

Charlotte looked down in consternation. Maybe Benny's death wasn't altogether an accident.

Dr. Woodford continued. "I've heard of such things before, of course, but they were always apocryphal or unattributed. Someone who heard from someone else, long ago...." She strolled a bit ahead, looking carefully left and right, and walked directly into a sap line and fell down. "Ooof," she said.

"Are you OK?" Charlotte called as she ran over.

"I'm fine, dear." She put her hand on the ground to help herself up and felt something lumpy. "What's this?"

Charlotte squatted next to Dr. Woodford. "Did

you find something?"

Dr. Woodford lifted her hand from the leaf litter, holding some woven bark scraps. "That looks a lot like the photo Chester sent me," Charlotte said, "but these look worn out." They brushed away the leaves, revealing a pile of decaying lines.

"Eureka," Dr. Woodford said.

"Wow, the jackpot!" Charlotte exclaimed. She quickly snapped a bunch of photos. "This will make an amazing story," she thought. She could already see the headline, Secret Society Steals Sap...

Dr. Woodford tugged hard on one of the lines, which unfortunately was running underneath Charlotte, whose feet were pulled out from under her, toppling her to the ground and ending her reverie. She landed alongside Dr. Woodford, who was closely examining the line. She pulled out a magnifying lens and looked closer. Charlotte got her camera out — luckily, not damaged in the fall — and took a great photo of Dr. Woodford's eye, doubly magnified by her thick lens and the magnifying glass.

"This is definitely not a commercial product," Dr. Woodford announced. "Look at this, it has all the hallmarks of primitive handiwork. But the complexity of the weave, and the nature of the material ... hmmm..."

"Whose work could it be?" Charlotte asked.

"Ah, that is the question, isn't it." Dr. Woodford cautiously extracted some of the lines from the pile and placed them carefully in a plastic bag. She stood up, obviously well pleased with the find. "This will provide an enormous amount of data for me to pursue. I wonder if I can get some time on the scanning electron microscope? And then there's radioisotope analysis, spectral imaging..." She began walking back through the woods towards her car, mumbling about research directions and grant possibilities. She had already forgotten that Charlotte was there.

"But what is it?" Charlotte called. Dr. Woodford waved without slowing down. "Scientists," Charlotte thought. She checked her watch. "Oh no," she thought, "I'd better get ready for tonight!" She ran off after Dr. Woodford, leaf litter flying under her feet, camera swinging around her neck.

Chapter 4

The band was playing up a storm. Charlotte tapped her foot in time with the heavy bass beat, the drummer providing a multirhythmic syncopated contrast, while the guitarist picked out variations of the theme. And the singer — what a voice, like elixir of rose petals strained through a velvet screen — crooned into the microphone about love lost and found and lost again, in an unending, imprisoning circle. It was bluesy and dark and smooth, and it filled the club with a warm vibe that went well with the wood paneling, the warm glow from the fireplace, and the local microbrews on tap.

Chester leaned close and said, "They're sounding good, honey." She nodded and smiled, touching his hand affectionately. She snuggled against him, resting her head on his shoulder. It had been a while since they had a night out, what with Chester's work and her late nights covering local meetings. And no creatures were chasing them. She snuggled closer, making the most of the evening.

They were sitting at a table near the stage, sharing a piece of pie and sipping coffee. Jimmy sat with them, nodding and tapping. He looked over at Chester and shouted, grinning widely, "They're tight tonight!" His girlfriend was the lead singer of the band, Dusty Rhoades and the Frost Heaves. As Dusty liked to say, they were world-famous in Vermont. They had a loyal following, though, and hoped one day to make enough money to give up their day jobs, or at least go on tour outside the state once in a while.

Dusty was a sight to behold, dressed in a fringed suede jacket over a low-cut white blouse, tight black jeans, and black boots. She was decorated with silver and turquoise bracelets, rings, and matching belt buckle. She had wavy long brunette hair that swung freely as she danced across the stage.

The Heaves were three brothers, the twins Paul and Jay, and the young one, Steve. They were dressed in similar dark outfits, black jeans and t-shirts. They didn't say much, but they played a mean lick together.

The song ended, and through the applause Dusty called out, "Are you ready for a sappy song?"

"Yes!" the audience shouted, Charlotte and Chester included.

"OK, here goes. A little Vermont variation on a famous jazz tune." The bass player began plucking out a lazy walking beat for four bars, then Dusty joined in, using a high-jazz drawl:

> Sugar time, and the living is easy,
> Sap is runnin', and the temperature's high,
> Your daddy's tappin', and your mamma is
>   cookin',
> And you, little baby, you ain't gonna cry...

The band continued playing while Dusty hummed the melody and danced around the stage. They were performing at The Hip Joint, a small club with old wood beams and a pressed tin roof. It was located on a quiet side street in St. Fred, a small town just down the hill from Skunk Hollow. Though by most urban standards St. Fred was nothing more than a rather tiny village, it was large enough to have a supermarket and a gas station, both open later than 8 PM, which was really something in that part of the state.

The club was named for the articulated skeleton that sat on a swing over the bar, kicking its leg out over the patrons. Chester thought the skeleton was kind of creepy. He stared at the kicking leg and felt himself getting hypnotized. He shook his head, trying to clear it.

The song ended with Dusty reprising the first verse, to loud applause. She called out, "Thanks, everyone, we'll be back soon. Go order another beer so they'll invite us back!" She jumped lightly off the stage and sat next to Jimmy.

"How'd we sound?" she asked him.

"Groovy, baby." She cuffed him on the shoulder. "You're a goofball. Give me a kiss," which he did, gladly. She reached over and grabbed some of his fries.

"You're singing well tonight, Dusty," Charlotte said. "You guys have such a great sound together."

Dusty swallowed the fries and said, "Thanks, Charlie. I missed an entrance, and I went flat a few times, but not too terrible."

Jimmy said, "Good enough for jazz, baby." She grimaced, then took some more fries.

"Are you working on anything exciting, Charlie?" Dusty mumbled around the fries. "Any lurking monsters?"

"Oh, just the usual grind," she answered. "It's not a very exciting town. How about you? Any good gigs coming up?" Charlotte was also the music reviewer for her paper.

Dusty swallowed and said, "There's Burning Moose this weekend, but otherwise just a few club dates around the state. I guess we haven't been discovered yet."

"You will be, I know it," Jimmy said. "You guys are the bee's knees."

"Doofus," she said as she leaned over and kissed him again.

Burning Moose was Skunk Hollow's answer to the Burning Man festival. They held the event in a clearing on top of Skunk Mountain, typically on a Saturday in mid-November, before it got too cold. Chester and his friends wove together dried corn stalks, fallen branches and straw into the shape of a 30-foot moose, poured grease from a local restaurant on top, and lit it at dusk. The blaze could be seen for miles around, and it burned for hours. It was always a challenge finding just the right distance from the bonfire so that one neither broiled nor froze. Besides the bonfire, local bands played for the crowd, and there was plenty of food and drink. Charlotte hoped to do a two-page spread on the festival, if the Publisher approved.

Charlotte's phone rang. She didn't recognize the caller. Chester leaned over and said, "It's probably one of those robo-calls. Just ignore it. Want more pie?"

She was tempted, but something about the call tugged at her. The caller's name was a strange sequence of numbers and letters, like the kind of thing she'd seen on her computer screen when she made the mistake of asking it for help. "Who knows," she thought, "maybe it's a lead." She decided to answer. "Hello?"

She heard loud static, with an underlying hum that rose and fell. It seemed like senseless noise, and she was ready to hang up, but then she stayed on. Maybe there was something there, possibly a deeper message? Chester, looked worried. "Everything OK, Charlie?"

Charlotte nodded, listening more closely. She realized there was a hum within the hum. The static seemed to be resolving into something else, not quite words, but some weird, extrasensory voice. She strained harder to listen. And then, suddenly, she understood it, like an optical illusion that suddenly snaps into clarity. "Leave...us...alone...don't...touch... us...let...us...be..."

It felt like she was tumbling, tumbling down a deep, dark well, like Alice down the rabbit hole, following the voice to its source. She could see a deep, dark tunnel ahead of her, a tunnel to the heart of the woods, twisting and turning. A shape began to resolve at the far end of the tunnel, silhouetted against the sky, large and imposing and somehow threatening, like those massive trees out west, sequoias, large enough to drive a car through, but that wasn't nearly as big as this tree. It was a vast and monstrous maple, and somehow it was growling out the words she heard through the static. It began thrashing around, as if a strong wind was blowing, but its movement had purpose. The gargantuan tree was reaching for her, its branches like arms, twigs like malevolent claws, and she was falling towards it, falling...

... and then she was on the floor. Chester's worried face was close as he leaned over her, cradling her head in his lap. Dusty and Jimmy were kneeling by her side, Dusty holding her hand, looking concerned. Jimmy heard noise and looked with surprise at the phone still gripped tightly in Charlotte's other hand, broadcasting static. "That's funny," he said.

"What is?" Chester asked, without taking his worried eyes off of Charlotte.

"That sounds like the noise our maple taps make. You know, the smart ones we put in today."

Charlotte sat up and said, "I saw it."

"What did you see?" Chester asked.

"A really big maple. And boy, was it angry!"

Chapter 5

Chester put another piece of wood into the stove and closed the cast-iron door. "There, that should do it," he said. Charlotte nodded but didn't look up. She was sitting sideways on her broken-down futon couch, the same one she had in her college dorm room, leaning her back against the arm, intent on her laptop computer screen. "This is good," she said, sipping spiced tea from a large mug Chester had served her.

Chester had driven Charlotte back to her tiny house in the woods after the call from the tree. He was hovering, concerned about any after effects from the fall or the weird phone call itself.

She looked up and said, "I really can't find

anything even remotely related to that strange call. And let me tell you, there are a lot of strange calls out there!"

"Maybe you should get a new phone," he said, looking askance at the offending device.

"Are you kidding? How many other cell phone plans include talking to trees? I'm keeping it." She looked up again and realized Chester was still worried. "I told you I'm fine, honey." She got a thoughtful look, and then, sneaking a look from the corner of her eye, she said, "You know, if you really want to protect me, maybe you could stay here more, move a few things in..."

"Now hold on there, Charlie, you know I love you, but living together is a big step, and I'm not sure the time is right yet, I mean,... um..."

"Oh, don't mind me, you know whatever you want is fine with me." She stared down at her lap, momentarily defeated, but then had an idea. "If you really want to help, you can start that massage you're always promising."

Chester sat at the other end of the couch and said, "As you wish." He lifted her left foot, took off her shoe and began massaging. Thinking out loud, he said, "It must have been some kind of crazy automated call, one of those tricky ones that try to hypnotize you so you'll give them all your personal information."

"No, it was definitely something else, something menacing," she said. "Don't forget the ankle. I think I twisted it in the forest today, chasing Dr. Woodford."

Chester focused on the offending joint. "But what could it be?" he said. "A big maple tree with a cell phone? It just doesn't make sense."

"I'm not so sure about that," she said. "Don't forget the other foot."

"Yes, dear."

She pressed a few keys on her laptop, bringing up a file. Leaning forward, she said earnestly, "Like here's a paper from Dr. Woodford about tree messaging."

"Um, tree messaging?" he asked, quizzically.

"You know, trees talking to each other, in their own way. A language, if you want to call it that. She's got evidence of communication between trees, like if you injure one by cutting off a branch, the closest one reaches over as if to comfort it."

"A tree hugger," Chester said, amused.

Charlotte lightly kicked Chester in the shoulder. "Don't scoff just because you've never noticed it. It takes a long time to happen, so you need one of those slow-motion time-lapse cameras to see it."

"Next you'll tell me they walk, too. Walking, talking, hugging trees. What next?" Chester said.

"Well, it's funny you asked," Charlotte said. Chester looked up at the ceiling, with a 'Why me?' expression. She moused around on her laptop until she found what she was looking for. "Like this paper here, where some scientist talks about a whole network of mycelium..."

"My ceiling gum?" Chester asked in surprise.

"No, mycelium," Charlotte insisted. "You know, mushroom fibers that grow underground. You've got them in your compost pile, if you ever bothered to turn it over. They stretch between the tree roots, letting them talk to each other. It's a fungal internet."

"That scientist must be a fun guy..." Chester said.

She lightly kicked him again. She looked down at her laptop and said, "And there's this other study..."

Chester leaned over and closed her laptop.

"What was that for?" Charlotte said in surprise. "I've still got so much research to do."

Chester grinned and said, "I'm sending a message." Reaching into his pocket, he pulled out a small gift-wrapped box. He handed it to her and blurted, "Happy anniversary!"

"Anniversary?" she said, looking puzzled. "But it's barely half a year since we met." She tore off the wrapping paper and popped open the box. Lying on cotton was a pair of golden earrings, in the shape of maple syrup jugs, with inscribed labels: "Sugar" on one, "Maple" on the other.

"That's right," he said. "It's been exactly six months since we, uh, met, and..."

"And you saved me, and we fell in love," she gushed. "My rustic Romeo!" She dove forward to hug him, sending the laptop flying and the mug of tea spinning in the air. With the power of centrifugal motion, the tea slopped over the rim and all over Chester's shirt and pants.

"Oh, no!" she cried. "What a mess!" She grabbed a napkin and started dabbing and blotting ineffectually at his shirt. "I've ruined our anniversary." She looked at the sodden Chester and said, "How can we save it?"

Chester took her wrist, pulled away the napkin, and lifted her hand to his mouth, planting a gentle kiss. He stood up and started to unbutton his sopping shirt, slowly. "I've got a few ideas," he said. "Happy anniversary."

"Oh, yes?" she said, leaning back on the couch with a twinkle in her eye. As the shirt dropped to the floor she whispered, "Oh, my!"

Chapter 6

Charlotte looked for an open space on the crowded picnic table to place her honey-maple chocolate chip cookies. It was already covered with plates and bowls and platters, filled with an astonishing assortment of desserts, like peach cobbler and chocolate brownies and every kind of pie and cake one could imagine. She shoved a double chocolate cake over a few inches and added her plate to the mix. "Here you go, Miss Beth," she said.

"Thank you, dear," Beth answered. "Do you see what she brought, Sharon?"

"Of course, Beth, we can always depend on our Charlotte for something delicious."

The sisters Elizabeth and Sharon Royalton were the doyennes of the dessert table. They saw to the sweets at every event in Skunk Hollow, and their pies were legendary. No one knew their age — they were retired school teachers — but they carried themselves with such elegance and aplomb, everyone called them Miss Beth and Miss Sharon, as if they were from a distant, more respectful time.

Charlotte looked around at the happy crowd. The whole town was there for the Burning Moose festival, gathered in the clearing on top of Skunk Mountain. She knew nearly all of them, and was related to at least half. The full spectrum of ages was represented, from toddlers to geriatrics, spanning the demographics of the town: aging hippies and ski bums, young families taking a well-deserved break from farm chores and child care, pale-looking office workers, plumbers and electricians, loggers and welders, a few local artists and sculptors who liked working in the country, and the heart of the town, the fifth-generation farmers in their overalls and boots, sitting in a circle in their camp chairs, drinking beers and telling tales. There was so much going on, it was like the carnival came to town, with ring toss and face painting for the kids, and plenty of drinks and snacks for the older crowd.

Charlotte waved at old Stoney Stubblefield, thin as a rail and older than Methuselah, holding down the burger and weenie grill, as usual. He waved back with his spatula, grinning. His even older and thinner brother, Snowy Stubblefield, was focused on rolling out dough and spreading toppings for stone-baked pizzas, his specialty.

Madge was doing a brisk business at the sausage booth, Charlotte saw. There was a banner across the front, with a photo of Benny eating a sausage sandwich, ketchup and grease dripping onto his shirt. He looked happy. "That's a fitting memorial," Charlotte thought.

Next to Madge was the booth for Artie's, the only restaurant in town, serving family style home cooking, which meant enormous portions of farmer favorites like meatloaf and potatoes covered in buckets of gravy. Printed on a banner above the booth was the restaurant's slogan, "We put the 'oat' in haute cuisine!" Artie himself, a rather rotund, cheerful large fellow in an apron and jacket, was greeting the customers while his numerous kin served the food.

Charlotte heard running. She turned and then jumped back to avoid being trampled by the Strudellpuff family -- Peter and Penny and their energetic children, Patricia and Patrick. They raced by, looking lean and lanky and kind of stringy, like marathon runners. They were just way too healthy. As they passed by, Penny shouted over her shoulder,

"One more trip up and down the mountain and we'll have a new personal best!" Charlotte felt out of shape just watching them run down the slope.

Way across the clearing was Jerky Dan, six foot plus, broad as a snow plow and strong as a tractor, selling his locally made jerkies. Beef jerky, of course, and jerked chicken, but also goat, venison, and even jerky somehow made from kale. Charlotte had briefly dated him way back when, but she could never get used to his habit of lifting her up and flinging her over his shoulder at the start of each date. He was doing a brisk business, but when he noticed Charlotte he winked.

Even Dr. Woodford was there. Charlotte watched as she carefully balanced a plate with burger and fries and navigated to one of the picnic tables. Surprisingly, she didn't drop more than a few fries.

Everyone looked like they were having fun on one of the last sort of sunny days before winter, Charlotte noted as she aimed her camera at the crowd. It wasn't exactly warm, but at least it wasn't freezing yet, and that in itself was reason to celebrate.

And then there was the music, performed live all day and into the night on a natural stage of large rocks, probably deposited by some retreating glacier ten thousand years ago. It seemed to Charlotte that almost everyone in town played some instrument. All the local musicians got to play a set, from the worst to the not too bad to the pretty good. Right now a group of surprisingly talented twelve-year-olds were performing bluegrass tunes on fiddle, banjo, and washtub bass.

Charlotte had been researching the history of the festival for her article. Burning Moose started as a silly prank around 15 years ago by a few teenagers who had nothing better to do in November. One of them found an old moose made out of woven branches, probably some backwoods art project that got repurposed for target practice, and for some reason the teens built a bonfire around it. They had beer and potato chips, and they played their old guitars, sang and danced until the fire burned out. Every year since, "that crazy moose event" attracted more and more people, and the moose kept getting larger, until this year it was nearly 30 feet high at the antlers.

Charlotte looked from the moose down the mountain at the town of Skunk Hollow, spread out below like a patchwork quilt. There wasn't much to the town, mostly sagging, weather-beaten old homes clustered around the town green, along with a couple of rundown churches, a gas station, Artie's restaurant, and a post office about the size of a postage stamp. The village center was surrounded by miles and miles of woods, mostly bare, but with stands of dark green pines on the stony hillsides and patches of yellowing tamaracks scattered throughout. Although the dairy industry had been declining for decades, a few farms struggled along, with their pastures and cornfields, rambling white farmhouses and ancient dairy barns a few decades past their last paint job. Threading through the woods was a twisting network of narrow dirt roads and electric and telephone lines that held the village together. You could gather the entire population in a small movie theater and still have room for a few football teams.

Charlotte loved this run-down, rustic place, and even if fame ever came her way she couldn't imagine living anywhere else. Now if Chester would get a little more serious about their living arrangements...

"Are these yours, Charlie?" Dusty said as she pushed by and reached for a cookie. She took a bite. "Yum! These are just soaked in maple syrup. They've gotta be yours."

"Yup, my usual contribution," Charlotte answered. "Are you ready for tonight?"

"Oh, sure," Dusty said through a mouthful of sweetness and crumbs. "We're gonna rock their socks. You'd better get some good pictures of me, so I have something to send to my agent."

"You have an agent?"

"Well, not yet, but you never know..."

"Have you seen Chester?" Charlotte asked, glancing around. "He seems to have vanished."

Dusty mumbled through another cookie, "I think he's hiding behind the moose."

Charlotte looked over and saw Chester standing on a ladder, leaning precariously out to touch the

moose's head. He was adjusting the antlers, shifting them up and down.

"I'd better see if he needs some help," she said. "See you later." She trotted over to the moose and called up, "A little to the left."

Chester, surprised, jumped and nearly fell off the ladder.

"Oh no!" Charlotte gasped.

Just as he was about to fall he grabbed the moose's head and hung from it, legs dangling. He swung back, regaining his balance on the ladder. "No problem," he called down, a bit shakily.

"I think the mouth needs to be tilted up a bit more," Jimmy said from the other side of the moose. "It looks like he's frowning at us."

Charlotte looked up and said, "You know, he does look a bit grumpy."

Chester carefully shifted a couple of branches. "That's it, bro, that's a happy moose!" Jimmy shouted. Charlotte nodded agreement.

"You sure?" Chester asked. "I don't want to climb up here again. Let's ask Mike, he has a good eye." He looked around. "Where did he go?"

"Mike's dogging it," Jimmy complained. "He's still worrying about those smart taps. Probably wandered over to tuck them in for the night."

Charlotte perked up. "Smart taps? Mike has some?"

Jimmy bragged, "He makes them! But he's not happy with them lately."

"Why not?" Charlotte asked.

"They've been acting a little weird." Jimmy scratched his head, then added, "It's like they're getting their own ideas. They turn on and off without any instructions. Mike said something about using packet sniffing to see what they're up to."

"Packet sniffing?" Charlotte wondered. "You mean like those drug-sniffing dogs at the border?"

"Nah, an app of some kind that looks at the data going from tap to tap. I guess the data goes in packets."

Jimmy paused and scratched his head again. "Mike said he's going to show them who's boss, whatever that means. I mean, they're just little computers, right?"

Charlotte frowned at Chester and said, "That doesn't sound very good."

Chapter 7

Mike was indeed trying to show the taps who was boss, but he wasn't having much luck. He was standing in the middle of the Skunk Mountain sugarbush, surrounded by sap lines, staring at a complicated packet-sniffing app on his phone. He was trying to see what kinds of messages the smart taps were sending over the network, and it wasn't looking good.

"No, no, no!" he scolded. "There's no animal threat there, why are you running current through that line?" He typed a few lines of code, adjusted a few sliders, pressed a few buttons, then waited to see the packets change. They didn't. There was still current running to places it shouldn't. Very high current.

He looked up at the offending taps and shouted, "You are not cooperating! I'm going to have to wipe your memory." He brought up a map of the nearby smart taps and began trying to reset them. But they weren't responding to that, either. "Maybe something's blocking the signal," he thought. He shifted a few feet over, held the phone up over his head, and tried a few other positions, all with no effect. He poked the phone hard and shouted, "Reset, I said!" Still no change.

He looked around for something to throw at a tap to get its attention when he noticed an odd, blind-like structure off to the right. "There shouldn't be anything there," he thought, "there's no hunting here." He walked over to get a better look.

The structure was built of bark, woven in rather intricate, delicate patterns and tied to four maples at its corners. It was definitely not a hunting blind, not with those woven windows, more like a rose arbor or garden bower. There was a bench in the back of the arbor, he noticed, made of a split log tied to two trees. He sat down and looked around. For some reason he felt at peace, something he rarely experienced.

Mike touched the wall to his right and felt the rough texture of the bark. It was artfully braided to form rope of a sort, with intricate knots tying the strands together, like macramé. "Whoever built this understood the woods," he thought. "It should be like this all the time." He felt himself drifting, almost dozing. "I could stay here forever," he thought, "serving the trees..."

He looked around in a daze, overwhelmed by the beauty of the forest, something he hadn't noticed in a very long time. Then he glanced down at his phone and saw that nothing had changed with the taps, breaking the spell. "Ah, well," he thought, "so much for peace." He stood up and sadly stepped out of the bower, heading back to the taps. This had gone on long enough. He pressed reset a few more times, without success.

"If that's the way you're going to be, I'll do a global reset," he muttered. He called up the master list of taps and found the "Reset All" button. "Here we go, you little troublemakers."

Before he could press the button, the phone rang. He looked around in surprise. Calls usually didn't get through in this cellular dead zone. A strange caller ID appeared, one he didn't recognize, but he answered anyway. "Hello?" he said.

There was no one on the line, only a loud, static-filled hum, which got progressively louder and higher pitched. It was hypnotic. A deeper hum joined in from the woods, in harmony with the phone. He looked around but couldn't pinpoint the source; it seemed to be coming from everywhere and nowhere, as if all the trees were moaning, from their roots to their highest branches. The sap lines began vibrating in tune with the hum, like a gigantic stringed instrument in a global orchestra. Something slithered on the forest floor, underneath the fallen leaves. He looked back at his cell phone screen and saw with horror that it was now crawling with wild pixels, unmoored from their locations.

The hum was driving him crazy. He closed his eyes tightly and put his hands over his ears, but the hum seemed to enter through his skin. He couldn't take much more of this. He was ready to give up and run. Just then something grabbed his ankle and tripped him, throwing him to the ground.

"No, you've got to listen to me!" he shouted. Snaking sap lines curled around his legs and climbed his body, joined by others that trapped his arms and wrapped around his chest. As Mike struggled helplessly, one sap line circled his neck and approached his ear. It held a smart tap at its end. The snaky line pushed the tap into his ear canal. He screamed, then suddenly, ominously, fell silent.

Mike lay there, inert, as the lines pulsed and squeezed. He wasn't dead, more like in stasis, immobile. Then the lines relaxed all at once, unwinding rapidly from his body and slithering away. The tap in his ear began to glow. At first it blinked in a simple pattern, which became more intricate and varied. Beneath his closed lids, Mike's eyes moved about in sync with the blinking.

His eyes snapped open. He tried to stand, fell, then tried again. He moved like he had forgotten how to use his limbs. After a few more tries he finally regained his feet. His eyes moved in a jerky, random pattern, and he appeared to be listening to some voice only he could hear. He took one stiff step, then another, moving like an automaton. He moved slowly and stiffly, plodding up the mountain, snaking sap lines trailing in his wake.

Chapter 8

It was dusk, and the festival was in full swing. Dusty's band was finally performing, playing some beat-heavy tunes, and a well-fed, nicely liquored crowd was dancing in front of the stage. Charlotte stood on a chair, trying to get a photograph, but even with the additional elevation she was still a bit too short to see over the crowd.

"Want to sit on the moose?" Chester asked. "He's tall enough. And he's not lit yet."

"Hmmm, maybe later..." she replied, distracted. "I just can't seem to capture the whole scene," she said, frowning at her latest shot.

"I know," Chester said, "why don't you sit on my shoulders. That should get you high enough."

"Good idea." Charlotte said. He squatted in front of her chair and she climbed on. "Upsy daisy," he said as he stood up.

"Whoa," she gasped as she grabbed his hair. "I'm going to get altitude sickness up here." He stood still until she relaxed. "That's much better." She put the camera to her eye and snapped away. "What a view!" she said. "I'm getting it all."

"Me too, Charlie, me too," Chester said, softly.

The group finished the song to a wave of applause. "Thanks, folks!" Dusty called into the mic. "Let's hear it for the best backup band in the world, the Frost Heaves!" A loud cheer went up as the brothers nodded, too shy to look at the audience.

Charlotte snapped some photos of the band. "Turn around, quick," she said to Chester, "I want to get the crowd applauding." Chester spun, almost flinging Charlotte off his shoulders. She grabbed his head again and said, "Hey, take it easy, I forgot my seat belt." She regained her balance and snapped away at the cheering throng.

"Here's another song for you," Dusty announced. "It will be on our first album, if we ever finish it... Anyway, maybe some of you gals out there can relate to this one. It's called 'When the Sap Starts Running'."

The crowd clapped and cheered. "I love this one!" Charlotte said to Chester. "Let me down." Chester squatted and she jumped off. She ran up to the stage, with Chester trailing behind.

The drummer started pounding the bass drum, the bass player joined in with a walking beat, and then the guitar played out a line of the chorus. Dusty nodded along, getting a fix on the rhythm, then started crooning:

> I'm just a cold and lonely little Green
>   Mountain girl
> Shiv'rin' in my PJs in a snow-covered world.
> Putting on the mittens,
> Wearing twenty layers or so...
> I wish I had some money and a cozy warm
>   place to go.

"I'll warm you up, Dusty!" some joker called out from the crowd. "I bet you'd try," she replied tartly.

> My boyfriend took his truck and headed
>   right out of town,
> He promised to come back for me once he
>   settled down.
> I'm waiting with my suitcase,
> Waiting for the phone to ring.
> But I hear he's down in Nashville and he
>   won't be back 'til spring.

"OK, here comes the chorus," Dusty called. "You can echo us on the second line."

> Now when the sap starts running,

The crowd shouted: "When the sap starts running!"

> Yes, when the sap starts running,
> I'm going to boil you down.

Loud cheering from the crowd. "That's right!"

someone called. "You get that stinker!"

"You better believe it," Dusty answered, with feeling.

> I've got my spouts and buckets and I'm ready
>   for the spring,
> That dirty rat is coming back and he's
>   looking for a fling,
> He says he missed me dearly,
> Missed me nearly every night,
> He thinks I'm sugar candy and everything
>   will soon be alright.
>
> But I've found a frosty fellow and he's happy
>   with the snow,
> His eyes are coal, his hat is silk, and he's got
>   nowhere to go,
> He says he'll stay all winter,
> He says he'll keep me warm,
> And he doesn't go a-runnin' when we've got
>   another storm.
>
> So when the sap starts running,
> (When the sap starts running)
> Oh, yeah, when the sap starts running,
> I'm going to boil you down.

The band repeated the chorus as Dusty danced. She ended with a heartfelt "I'm gonna boil you down!" The crowd erupted into applause. "More!" they yelled. "You tell 'im, Dusty!"

"We're Dusty Rhoades and the Frost Heaves," she called out. "See you at the dessert table!"

Jimmy ran up to the stage and whispered

something to her. "Hold on, folks, it's time to light the moose!" She turned to the band and said, "Let's get some moose music going here."

The Frost Heaves started playing something moose-like, while Chester raced Jimmy to the massive structure. Charlotte was right behind, trying to get in position to photograph the lighting. "This is so exciting!" she called out. Chester looked back and smiled, then sprinted to the finish, just beating Jimmy. The rest of the crowd gathered around in a big semi-circle, with excited children jumping up and down.

"No pushin' now, it's gonna git hot," Snowy Stubblefield warned.

Chester grabbed a long branch with straw wrapped around the end, soaked in cooking grease. Jimmy took out a match and said, "Ready?"

"Light it," Chester commanded.

The torch burst into flame with an admirable flash. Chester carefully lifted it up to the moose's belly. "Here we go!" Jimmy yelled. The crowd held its collective breath.

The torch barely touched the belly of the beast when, with an explosive whoosh, the moose caught. A loud cheer went up. The fire spread rapidly to the rest of the structure, sending out a wave of heat that pushed everyone back.

The children jumped and screamed in joy, and there were oohs and ahs from the adults. Even the teens, who'd already seen it all, looked enthralled. "That's the way to do it," Jimmy said to Chester, patting him on the back. Charlotte was photographing people dancing in front of the burning moose. "Another good one," she called out to

Chester. Jimmy gave her a thumbs up.

People shuffled forward and back, trying to avoid incineration and yet keep warm in the cooling night.

Chester took a step back and put his arm around Charlotte. She said, "You sure know how to light a fire."

He looked deeply into her eyes and said, "Speaking of fire..."

"Yes?" she whispered, breathlessly.

As Chester leaned close, they heard rustling and slithering in the shrubs to the right of the moose. "What's that?" Charlotte asked worriedly.

"Probably just a spooked fox," Chester reassured her. "Or a raccoon. Maybe even a small black bear. Or a bobcat. I saw one up here the other day."

"Is that supposed to make me feel better?" she said.

The rustling noises got louder. Charlotte could see the bushes shaking. And then she noticed something slithering in the undergrowth. "Snakes?" she asked in

a trembling voice.

"Harmless ones, most likely," Chester said, though he wasn't so sure. He held her a bit tighter.

Mike staggered into the clearing, trailed by the snaking sap lines. His eyes glowed red, reflecting the fire. The spout in his ear blinked a complex pattern. Jimmy ran over and said, "Mike, where've you been?"

Still in a trance, Mike grabbed Jimmy and lifted him off the ground effortlessly. "What are you doing, Mike?" Jimmy yelled. Mike tossed him aside, luckily away from the fire. A sap line slithered rapidly over and pinned Jimmy to the ground, while other lines approached menacingly.

"Hey, man," Jimmy yelled, "get this off me!"

"Mike!" Chester shouted. "What are you doing? Jimmy's your best friend."

Mike turned to face Chester and walked stiffly towards him. "Go away," Mike said in a mechanical monotone. "Leave us alone. These woods are not yours to burn."

No one else had noticed the disturbance yet. Everyone was intent on the bonfire, until one of the children pointed, pulling her mother's arm. "Look, a blinking man," she said.

"Oh my god! What's happened to Mike and Jimmy?" her mother shouted. Others turned and noticed the disturbance. Some stepped forward to see better, others backed away. The band, finally noticing something wrong, played a few off notes and then stopped. Dusty stopped singing, with her mouth hanging open.

Mike approached Chester, pointing at him and chanting, "Go away, go away, go away..."

Charlotte jumped in front of Chester to protect

him. "You keep away from my boyfriend. We just celebrated our half-year anniversary!"

Chester took a step forward and stood alongside her. He put his arm around her shoulder protectively and said, "You'd better listen to her, Mike, she means business."

Mike halted. He was so still, it looked to Charlotte that no one was home. There was only a faint pulse beating in his throat, in time to the blinking light at his ear. Then he slowly shifted, moving slightly. He raised his arm and pointed at Charlotte and Chester. "Get them," he ordered in a soft, menacing voice. The sap lines slithered forward rapidly. Before the terrified couple could move, the sap lines trapped them, effectively wrapping them together. Charlotte lost her balance and they tumbled to the ground.

Mike stood over the struggling couple and spoke to everyone. "This is what awaits you all. Leave us alone or face the same fate." More sap lines appeared, threatening them with taps. There were cries of fear.

Out of the terrified crowd stepped Dr. Woodford. She looked even more diminutive than usual. But there was grandeur in her face and gravitas in her bearing. She walked fearlessly towards Mike, stopping just a few feet before him. "I know what you want," she said.

"How can you know, poor human, with your short and isolated life," Mike said.

"You want what any tree wants. To grow, to reach for the sky, to burrow deep into the earth."

"Yes," said Mike.

Dr. Woodford stepped back and began to intone an odd and magical poem:

We are the Trees.
Our dark and leafy glade
Bands the bright earth with softer mysteries.
Beneath us changed and tamed the seasons
     run:
In burning zones, we build against the sun
Long centuries of shade.

Mike sighed deeply. The sap lines seemed mesmerized by her words. Dr. Woodford stood taller and continued:

We are the Trees
Who bear him company
In life and death. His happy sylvan ease
He wins through us; through us, his cities
     spread
That like a forest guard his unfenced head
'Gainst storm and bitter sky.

Her voice trailed away with the last line. Except for the crackling of the fire, there was silence that seemed to go on for a long time. Finally, Mike stirred and said, "Human, you understand."

"Yes," Dr. Woodford said. "We are not enemies. We are friends, partners, working together."

"Friends," Mike echoed.

"Though we take your sap, we also protect you, help you, raise you from a sapling until you cover the earth with your wide-reaching crown."

Tears formed in Mike's eyes. The sap lines, formerly so threatening, seemed as tame as young puppies.

"Um, friend?" Charlotte asked in a tiny voice.

"Could you release us?"

Mike looked at the entwined Charlotte and Chester, and at poor Jimmy, who was fighting off a sap line holding a tap near his head.

"Release them," he ordered. The sap lines went limp and collapsed to the ground. With a collective sniff they slithered away and vanished in the undergrowth.

Charlotte stood and helped Chester up. As they brushed each other off, Jimmy jumped up, finally free of the lines. He reached out and grabbed the smart tap in Mike's ear, and with a mighty twist he pulled it out. Mike crumpled to the ground. Jimmy threw the tap at the moose, embedding it in its burning flank. The crimson light blinked faster and faster, increasing its rate as the temperature rose, until it blinked so fast it seemed a solid, glowing thing. Then it slowly faded, becoming dimmer and darker until it was black.

Chapter 9

Charlotte was sitting cross-legged on her sagging couch, her laptop precariously balanced on her knees, putting the final touches on her news story. "How's Mike doing?" she asked.

"I don't know," Chester replied, carrying two beers from the kitchenette. "The doctors think he's completely recovered, but..."

Charlotte typed a few more words and then said, "Done! If this one doesn't get me nominated for a Pulitzer, I don't know what will." She sent off the article and asked, "But what? He's out of the hospital, right? He must be better."

Chester handed Charlotte one of the bottles and squeezed onto the couch next to her.

"There's just something different about him. It takes him longer to answer when I talk to him, and he often gets a far-away look. Like he's seeing... I don't know, into a different world."

"That makes sense to me," Charlotte said. "When you've shared your head with a bunch of angry maples, it's bound to change your point of view." She took a sip and began coughing. "What is this stuff?" she asked.

"Maple beer. It's made from fermented sap, with some hops and ground acorns and birch bark and things like that. Mike gave Jimmy the recipe. How do you like it?"

Charlotte took another sip, coughed a bit less, and said, "Um, it's got... potential..."

"Mike's got all sorts of new ideas," Chester enthused. "The trees are helping him build garden bowers like the one he found in the woods. And he's got a plan to use the woven sap lines to bring high-speed internet to all the houses in town, even those too far from the phone lines." He looked around Charlotte's apartment. "Even your tiny house here in the middle of nowhere."

"Middle of nowhere?!" Charlotte objected. "I'd like you to know, mister, that this little house once played a key role in the social life of the village. Why, they used to roll back the carpets and host weekly dances here way back when."

Chester looked around the house, from the combination living room/bedroom/den where they were sitting, to the kitchenette behind them, with the claw-footed bathtub next to the stove, to the miniscule bathroom just beyond the tub. "How many people could dance in here?" he wondered. "Two? Or were people that much smaller 'way back when'?"

Charlotte stood abruptly and walked over to the plank and cinderblock bookshelves by the door.

"Hey, wait a minute, Charlie, I was only kidding. It's a very nice house."

She kept her back to him as she fiddled with things on the upper shelf. He heard a click, followed by the sound of old fashioned music, like from a 1940s dance hall. She turned around slowly to face him. "Let's see," she said.

Puzzlement was replaced by understanding. He stood, bowed deeply and asked, "May I have this dance, ma'am?"

She curtsied and replied, "Why, of course, sir." Chester held up his left hand, which Charlotte grabbed with her right, and he put his right arm properly around her waist. She placed her left hand on his shoulder, and then they were off, dancing some kind of slow waltz-like thing, only occasionally bumping into the furniture.

"You dance divinely, sir," she said, as she rested her head against his shoulder. He smiled and pulled her closer. Then, daringly, he attempted a turn, but halfway through, Charlotte, stepping backwards, tripped over a throw rug and tumbled onto the couch, pulling Chester down on top of her. With startled eyes they looked at each other, then laughed. "Fred and Ginger we're not," she said.

They laughed some more, and one thing led to another as they got cozy on the couch. But then Charlotte heard a noise and froze.

"What's that?" she whispered. "Is that rustling coming from outside?"

"Probably just the wind." Chester said. "Or a

family of voles digging a new tunnel under the house. Or maybe it's..."

She covered his mouth with her hand. The rustling sounds got louder and closer. "Oh, no, it's happening again!" she squealed.

Chester jumped up and strode to the door, Charlotte tiptoeing behind. He opened the door a crack and they both peeked through the gap. In the dim light illuminating the sagging porch and the space beyond there was nothing much to see, just the usual collection of flower pots, barbecue grill, worn outdoor furniture and the like. But there was something happening in the bushes, just at the limits of the porch light, causing them to quiver and shake. A woven sap line appeared, and then another and another. Soon there was a whole collection of them.

And then a person crashed through the bushes, trailing even more lines.

"It's Dr. Woodford!" Charlotte exclaimed. "We've got to save her!" She pulled open the door, ready to jump to the good doctor's rescue.

"Oh, no dear, that's not necessary," Dr. Woodford calmly replied. She sat down on one of the rickety porch chairs, the sap lines gathering around her feet and ankles, gently caressing them. Chester noted with horror that Dr. Woodford had a smart tap in her ear, blinking its red light.

"But what about... that tap..." Chester said.

"Merely a research tool, some shared technology," she responded. "I'm gathering more data than ever before. And my powers of observation, they're... well... branching out in new directions. I've begun to learn the trees' natural language, speaking it in real time, without having to translate. If you'd like, I can wire you up, so to speak."

"Um, we're good," Charlotte said.

"Then good night, dear. I have so much more to learn." She stood and said, "I shall see you down the metaphorical road." And with that walked into the forest, sap lines trailing, as she recited:

> The woods are lovely, dark and deep.
> But I have promises to keep,
> And miles to go before I sleep,
> And miles to go before I sleep.

Her voice faded away on the last line. Chester quietly closed the door. He looked up at the ceiling, struggling to find the right words.

"You know, Charlie, it's not really safe for you out here. I mean, you never know what's going to come along and cause trouble... maybe something will try to carry you off again, or... you know..."

Charlotte looked up at Chester, wonderingly. "Why, what do you have in mind?" she asked coquettishly. "A security service? My own officer on call?"

"Um... maybe I should stay here more often. You know, maybe... um..."

"Move in?"

He gulped, nodded.

"Sweetheart!" she hollered as she threw her arms around him. She whispered into his ear, "Took you long enough." She looked deeply into his eyes, making sure he meant what he said. He raised his head and met her look bravely. She took his hand and led him back to the couch, when once more she heard sounds coming from outside. She stopped in her tracks. "Not again," she whimpered.

"I'm sure the trees are on our side now, Charlie. It's probably Dr. Woodford doing some more research." He took her worried face in his hands and kissed her gently. "I'll just take one more look and make sure it's safe. You get ready..."

"For sleep?" she asked, feigning ignorance.

"Something like that," he answered.

Charlotte quickly unfolded the couch into a bed and threw some sheets and blankets onto it, while Chester tiptoed to the door and peeked out. To his surprise, he saw Mike standing on a ladder, running sap lines to the breaker box.

"Mike," he hissed. "What are you doing? It's nearly midnight!"

"Just thought I'd connect up one more house." He tied another sap line to the TV antenna. "There, that should do it."

"Do what?"

"Why, high-speed internet, Ches. You know, the holy grail for Vermont. These trees may move slowly, but they still move faster than our government." He climbed down the ladder, looked at some readout on his phone and said, "Right, that's it. See ya, Ches."

"Bye, Mike." Chester walked back in to the house, shaking his head. Charlotte called from the bed, "Who was that?"

"Oh, just Mike, running more sap lines."

"Now?"

"You know Mike."

Chester threw off most of his clothes and joined Charlotte. "See," she said, as she snuggled against him, "it's not so bad living here." Chester held her close, and was getting ready for some more snuggling, when the TV snapped on with a loud musical fanfare, trumpets blazing and drums crashing. They sat up in shock and amazement. An announcer, who looked like an animated tree, bellowed, "WELCOME TO WSAP TV! ALL TREES, ALL THE TIME! AND NOW THE LATEST ARBOREAL NEWS!"

As the announcer continued his shouting, Charlotte desperately grabbed for the remote and started clicking buttons, with no effect. "Oh, no!" she cried, as she buried her head under her pillow. Chester ran to the door, threw it open and shouted, "Mike, I'm going to get you!!"